"Are you asking me to pose as your date?"

"What other reason would we have for being in Palermo together? I think it's the most believable scenario, don't you?"

Maybe it was the fatigue of the past twenty-four hours catching up with her, but Dara felt a wave of hysterical laughter threatening to bubble up to the surface. The thought that anyone would believe a man like Leo Valente was dating a plain Irish nobody like her was absolutely ludicrous.

He continued, oblivious to her stunned reaction. "You would leave the business talk to me. All I need is for you to act as a buffer of sorts—play on your history with Lucchesi's family. Someone with a personal connection to smooth the way."

"A buffer? That sounds *so* flattering..." she muttered.

"You would get all the benefits of being my companion and being a guest at an exclusive event. It would be enjoyable, I believe."

"Umberto Lucchesi is a powerful man. He must have good reason not to trust you," she mused. "I'm not quite sure I can risk my reputation."

"I'm a powerful man, Dara. You climbed a building to get a meeting with me. I'm offering you an opportunity to get exactly what you want. It's up to you if you take it or not."

Dear Reader,

This story began as a flicker of an idea—as most stories do. I was newly engaged and exploring a wedding fair in Dublin when I spotted a kiosk that advertised dream Italian weddings. The idea that someone could have such a glamorous job—planning events in such spectacular locations—was fascinating. The character of Dara was born instantly: a superorganized wedding planner on a mission to take her career to the next level.

It was while researching possible locations that I stumbled across the breathtaking Castello di Donnafugata in Ragusa. Leo's family estate is inspired by this ancient Sicilian landmark. I fell in love with the dramatic facade and wondered what it would have been like to grow up in such a place...to wake up in the morning and look out the arched windows to see waves crashing on the cliffs below...

And so it came about that I entered the 2014 *So You Think You Can Write* competition with the aim of finally typing *The End* on Leo and Dara's story. I had no idea that it would be the beginning of a wonderful adventure of my own. The support I received was overwhelming, and being named winner of the competition is a moment I will never, ever forget.

Writing, to me, is like dreaming on paper, and I am honored to be able to share my dreams with you.

Amanda

Amanda Cinelli

Resisting the Sicilian Playboy

Resisting the Sicilian Playboy

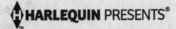

Recycling programs
for this product may
not exist in your area.

ISBN-13: 978-0-373-13859-3

Resisting the Sicilian Playboy

First North American Publication 2015

Copyright © 2015 by Amanda Cinelli

Printed in U.S.A.

www.Harlequin.com

Amanda Cinelli was raised in a large Irish/Italian family in the suburbs of Dublin, Ireland. Her love of romance was inspired after "borrowing" one of her mother's beloved Harlequin novels at the age of twelve. Writing soon became a necessary outlet for her wildly overactive imagination.

Now married with a daughter of her own, she splits her time between changing nappies, studying psychology and writing love stories.

For my dear friend Kirsty. This story
would never have been finished without you.

For my mother, Audrey. For your unwavering
belief in me, even when I didn't believe in myself.

And for my father, Paolo. For showing me
that with hard work and determination
you can achieve anything.

CHAPTER ONE

Dara Devlin had found herself in a few sticky situations in this job, but this had to be by far the worst.

A professional event planner should never gatecrash. It had to be written somewhere in the company handbook. Yet here she was, straddling the second-floor balcony ledge of Milan's most exclusive nightclub in four-inch designer heels.

All in the name of business, of course.

The heels had certainly slowed progress up the slippery emergency ladder, but leaving them in the alley below was unthinkable. A woman stood by her shoes, no matter how sticky the situation. And this situation most definitely qualified as *sticky*.

Handbag in one hand, she silently willed her skirt not to tear as she manoeuvred herself less than gracefully over the cold stone ledge, landing on hard marble tiles. Her watch showed it was just past ten. An unfashionably early time to be going clubbing in this part of the world, but dancing wasn't on her agenda tonight.

The city's premier celebrity hotspot, Platinum I, was celebrating its grand reopening this weekend and entry was strictly invitation only. No amount of her Irish charm would sway the arrogant hostess with her little black clipboard.

Nevertheless, Dara was determined to get into this party one way or another. She was only in town for the weekend before she had to head back south to her company's office in Syracuse. Failing this task just wasn't an option.

When her various contacts had said Leonardo Valente was untouchable, she had accepted the challenge with enthusiasm. She had the opportunity to plan the most high-profile wedding of her career—all she needed was one man's cooperation.

How hard could it be?

Even after three weeks of rejected emails

and dead-end phone calls she had refused to give up. Armed with her tablet computer and her snazziest designer suit, she had foolishly believed she could just travel to his Milan office and demand to be seen.

The joke was on her. Because it seemed that Leonardo Valente's office didn't even exist. The address on his secretary's email had led her to a professional call-answering headquarters, where her enquiries had all been rejected point-blank.

It was just plain good luck that she had found out about tonight. The first club in the worldwide Platinum chain was turning ten years old and celebrating with a star-studded relaunch weekend.

Her grasp on the Italian language was far from perfect, but one thing was certain: Leonardo Valente was here tonight, inside these walls. All she had to do was find a way inside.

She looked around the empty terrace and felt her stomach tighten. She had hoped it would be some sort of outdoor seating area where she could just climb over the wall and melt into the crowd. She bit her lip. It was still some part of the club, and it was her only hope of getting inside.

The wall of the building was made almost entirely out of glass, each pane a deep glossy black, making it impossible to see what was inside. The thump of music had been deafening down on the ground, but on this terrace it was completely muffled.

She ignored the uncomfortable twitch in her stomach, putting it down to nerves. She was sneaking into an exclusive event, after all—nerves were to be expected. In life sometimes you had to break the rules to get ahead, but this pretty much went against every fibre of her goody-two-shoes nature.

Pushing a strand of blonde hair from her face, she placed one hand on the window. Her pale skin reflected brightly in the black glass, her steel-grey eyes calm and focused as she made her way slowly from pane to pane. She began pressing her fingertips along each narrow gap, searching for a hinge, a hook—something that hinted at an opening.

After she had exhausted every possible angle, she stepped back and surveyed the rest of the terrace with a frown. It made no sense. Surely there had to be a way to get inside.

She felt a sudden irrational urge to kick the glass and force her way in. But that would never do. Dara Devlin quite simply did not lose her cool—no matter how rough the situation was getting. It was the main reason brides from all over the world called her to plan their dream Sicilian weddings.

With a deep, calming breath, she forced herself to think. While climbing up here had definitely been worth a shot, unfortunately she was now two storeys up and not going anywhere fast. Her hands gripped the cold stone as she peered over the ledge. The street looked much further down from up here, and she was suddenly feeling a lot less brave.

'*Signorina*, is there a particular reason you are sneaking around out here in the darkness?'

The deep, sensual voice came suddenly from behind her, making her breath catch painfully in her throat.

Dara turned slowly, eyes widening when

she saw that a pane of glass had somehow disappeared and a man now stood watching her.

How had she not heard someone coming? It was far too late to try and escape back down the ladder now. Her mind raced as she tried to find a way to spin this that wouldn't get her arrested.

'I'm waiting for an explanation.'

His face was slightly obscured in the shadows, but she could tell from his dark suit and crossed arms that he was definitely someone in charge—most likely Security. Damn and double damn. This was not going well.

Time to think, Devlin. Forcing her tone to keep light, she laughed breathlessly and spoke in fast-paced English. No one arrested a silly blonde in trouble.

'Well, finally someone's bothered to come out and help me.' She sighed for dramatic effect. 'I've been banging on the glass for twenty minutes, trying to get back inside.'

'You couldn't find the door, no?'

His perfect English surprised her, but the

mocking tone said he wasn't buying it. She kept talking anyway.

'It's a safety hazard. I was looking to get some fresh air and someone said I could step out here for a moment—'

'So you decided to scale the building to get to it?' he said. It wasn't a question, more an amused statement. 'Do you make a habit of wearing heels to climb up buildings? It's quite a talent.'

Dara opened her mouth to protest, but thought against it.

'One-way glass.' He gestured over his shoulder. It was too dark to see his face, but there was a definite smirk in his silky voice as he spoke. 'The moment you realised you weren't getting inside was really quite entertaining. I was convinced you were about to throw a tantrum.'

Dara huffed out the breath she hadn't even realised she had been holding. Well, it was great that he found this situation so funny, because from where she was standing her mission had just been unceremoniously called to a halt. She would likely be hauled out of here by the collar of her crisp white shirt and maybe even charged with trespassing.

'I realise how this looks—' she began, trying to keep the panic out of her voice.

'Do you? Because from here it looks like you were trying to break into my private floor in what I can only assume is a naughty secretary outfit.'

Dara frowned at that. 'What? I am *not* a naughty—' Her brain froze, processing the first chunk of his accusations.

The man stepped forward into the light, revealing a face that she had seen countless times in the tabloids. Dara felt her entire body freeze as she realised just who she had been lying to.

'Oh, God, you're him.'

Her razor-sharp professional reflexes turned to mush as she took in all six-feet-plus of muscular Sicilian male.

'If by "him" you mean the owner of the building you just attempted to break into, then that's a yes.' The glow seemed to have left his eyes now, and had been replaced by a keen cynicism. 'I suppose you're going to want to come inside now? Start telling

me about how this is all some crazy mis-
understanding?'

Arms folded across an impressive chest,
he stood waiting for her to dig her hole
even deeper.

Hot embarrassment clawed up Dara's
neck. He clearly thought this was a scheme
to get him alone. She'd read the magazines.
Women threw themselves at Leo Valente
everywhere he went. And it wasn't just
that he was mega-rich—although for some
women that would be more than enough.
With this man, the words they used were
mouthwatering, delicious and *sinful*.

It had always made her laugh to hear
of men described like desserts, but now,
standing five feet away from him, she
could kind of understand the madness.

He was a far cry from her usual type.
His dark hair reached just under his collar and was a bit too untidy, his eyelashes
were too long and his jaw overgrown with
dark stubble. But even she couldn't argue
that he was a sight to behold. And he had
taken one look at her tidy blazer and blouse

and presumed she was some groupie, here to play dress-up games.

She almost groaned with embarrassment. This was *not* the shining first impression she had banked on.

'Well, as much as I enjoy being stared at, I really don't have all night.'

Dara's heart gave an uncomfortable thump. 'I wasn't staring,' she said, rather too quickly. 'I was just…thinking.'

Oh, now this was just getting worse and worse. The moment she had been working towards for three weeks had finally presented itself and her mind had decided to go into sleep mode.

One dark eyebrow rose, mocking her. 'Were you thinking about this particular situation, or are there other criminal acts you've committed tonight?'

Criminal? Dara felt hot panic rise in her chest. 'Mr Valente, I can assure you I was not attempting to commit a crime.'

'Relax. I won't call in the hounds just yet. But you failed to notice the security camera watching your every move.' He pointed to a tiny blinking red light above her head. 'My team was halfway up here when I told them to wait.'

'Why did you do that?' The question was out before she could stop herself.

He shrugged one shoulder. 'I was bored. You looked interesting.'

She thought for a moment, but could not come up with a single response to that comment. Perhaps if he found her so interesting she could captivate him long enough to make her proposal.

She cleared her throat. 'Just so we're clear: I'm not a criminal. I'm a wedding planner.' She watched as his eyes narrowed.

'Same thing, in my opinion.' He smirked. 'I liked my naughty secretary theory much better.'

And just like that Dara found herself the subject of Leonardo Valente's infamous smouldering gaze. She cleared her throat, trying to think of something—anything—to break the tension. The air was beginning to feel very thin up here on this darkened terrace, and it had nothing to do with the altitude.

'Your theory is incorrect. I'm not here for anything like…like that.'

'Such a pity. Nonetheless, you have my attention.' He turned abruptly to go inside, pausing when she didn't immediately follow behind him. 'Unless you plan on going back down that ladder again, I suggest you follow me.'

With that he was gone, leaving Dara with no choice but to obey.

The room on the other side of the glass was twice the size of her entire apartment. She saw him press a few buttons in a panel on the wall and suddenly soft light illuminated the room. It was not an office, but nor was it an apartment. It reminded her of the lobby of a very exclusive hotel, with modern cubic seating and an impressive glass fireplace.

Exactly why a nightclub needed a room like this she wasn't sure—maybe he used it to entertain private guests. That thought made her clutch her handbag a little tighter in front of her, and feeling the outline of her computer reminded her of why she was there.

He pressed another button on the panel and the clever door slid silently back into place behind him. She could see that it was indeed one-way glass, and her ears burned at the thought of him watching her for all that time.

He turned around to face her and for the first time she noticed the vivid colour of his eyes. They weren't dark, as she had thought from his photographs, but a unique shade of deep forest green. Dara shook her head. Why was she even looking at his eyes, for goodness' sake? This was a business meeting, not a school dance.

'So, do you have a name—or will I just call you Spiderwoman?' That smirk was still firmly in place as he took a couple of steps towards her.

Her inner professional was sharp enough to see a perfect moment. 'I actually have my card in here somewhere…if you'd just give me a second…' She began fishing in her bag—maybe she should launch into the entire presentation now, before he had a chance to shoot her down.

Without warning he was in front of her,

taking the bag from her hand and placing it gently on the floor. 'I did not ask for a card. I asked for your name—from your lips, preferably.'

His gaze travelled down to her mouth and she felt her stomach flutter in response. She ignored the sensation, straightening her chin and meeting his gaze head-on. 'It's Dara Devlin.'

He nodded, as though she had answered correctly.

'So… Dara the wedding planner…' His deep voice purred her name, as though he was tasting it on his tongue. 'What gives me the pleasure of your company this evening?'

'I'm not here for pleasure.' She took a step back, wanting to put as much distance between them as possible. 'What I mean is, I came here to find you. To talk business.'

He raised one dark brow. 'Who comes to a nightclub to talk business?'

'Well, *you* do,' she said confidently. That earned her a puzzled look. 'I'm here to discuss a possible deal between you and a very high-profile client of mine.

All I'm asking is just five minutes of your time.'

'I have a swarm of media vultures downstairs in the club. Every one of them is waiting for "just five minutes". Why should you get to skip the queue?'

'If they deserved the time they would have climbed up here by now.'

Without warning he threw his dark head back and laughed—a deep, rumbling laugh that seemed to resonate right to her core. The gesture shocked her for a moment, and her eyes moved down to take in the strong column of his throat, the dark hairs that disappeared into the casually open collar of his shirt.

Dara swallowed, her throat feeling strangely dry. She looked up—only to be pinned by that mocking emerald gaze again.

'You know, despite the fact that you could have killed yourself climbing up here tonight, I admit that I'm impressed,' he said. 'You deserve those five minutes based on sheer nerve and creativity.'

Dara smiled with triumph and eagerly reached for the tablet computer in her bag.

'Wonderful. I've actually prepared a short pitch, if you want to take a seat?'

'No,' he said simply.

Her bag flopped back down to the ground as she took in his sudden change of tone. 'But you said that—'

'I said I'd give you your five minutes, Dara Devlin. I didn't say when.'

She felt a frown crease her forehead and quickly smoothed it down. This man was impossible. It was just five minutes, for goodness' sake. They had easily spent three times that up here already.

He gestured for her to move towards the door, closing a button on his tailored suit jacket in the process. 'You can arrange a time with my secretary. In the meantime, the party is just getting started downstairs.'

Dara felt her temper finally bubble up to the surface. 'I've been calling your secretary for three weeks—why do you think I pulled this stunt?'

'I just presumed you enjoyed a little espionage on a Friday night.' He smirked.

She fought the urge to stamp her foot in frustration. She needed to get to the subject of this meeting, but it had to be done just right or he would shoot her down—just like all the others who had approached him before her. Her presentation built up slowly, allowing her time to sway his thinking. He clearly wasn't going to give her that chance.

'Aren't you just a little curious about what made me climb up here?' she asked, desperate to stall him.

He moved forward so that they stood little more than a couple of steps apart in the silent room. 'It surprises me to find that I'm quite intrigued by you.' His eyes lowered to take in every inch of her body in one heated sweep.

Dara felt a rush of heat colour her cheeks. She might not have much experience with flirtation, but there was no mistaking the glitter in his eyes. This man was everything the tabloids made him out to be. Suave, sensual and utterly scandalous.

'You know, I can't remember the last time I made a woman blush.' He stepped closer, his voice deepening. 'Come have a drink with me, Dara. Let down that beautiful blonde hair of yours.'

'I don't think that would be appropriate, Mr Valente.' She pushed a tendril of hair behind her ear, feeling more than a little self-conscious under his gaze.

'Mr Valente was my father—you can call me Leo.' He smiled. 'What business could be so important that it can't wait until Monday morning?'

Dara spied her chance to turn the conversation. 'My condolences on your father's recent passing. I understand the funeral was held at your *castello* in Ragusa?'

'So I've been told.' He shrugged. 'People die every day, Miss Devlin. I prefer to focus on more enjoyable pursuits.'

Even after bringing up the subject of his father, the man was still flirting with her. He really was a complete playboy. She decided a more direct approach was definitely needed.

'The *castello* is a beautiful piece of history. It's such a shame that it lies dormant most of the time.'

'Why do I get the feeling this is more than idle chit-chat?' He narrowed his gaze, all trace of flirtation gone.

'Well, you see, it's part of the reason that I'm here.' Feeling a sense of foreboding, she powered on. 'I'm here to propose a deal for Castello Bellamo that I feel you will benefit greatly from.'

She blurted it out as confidently as she could and felt the swell of victory as he froze in place. The playful charmer seemed to disappear before her eyes, his expression taking on a detached hardness.

He met her eyes, a single muscle ticking on his jaw. When he spoke his voice was somehow deeper than before, his accent more pronounced. 'Well, it seems you have wasted both your time and mine tonight. I'll tell you the same thing that I have told every other vulture that has approached me since my father's death. The castle is not for sale.'

Dara shook her head, desperate for him to understand. 'I don't want to buy it—I want to hold a wedding there. I'm sure that we can come to some sort of—'

A flick of his hand cut her off mid-sentence. 'I don't care if you want to use it to house blind orphans. The matter is not open for discussion.'

'I understand that the *castello* has been left in disrepair for some time now—'

'It can stay that way, for all I care. Contrary to what people may think, these little games don't work for me—no matter how pretty the messenger is.' His eyes raked down to her heels, taking in every inch of her body with an exaggerated slowness before meeting her eyes once more.

'This conversation is over,' he gritted. 'I'll have someone sent up to escort you out. Now, if you'll excuse me, I've got a party to attend to.'

Without another word he strode from the room, leaving Dara to stare after him in disbelief.

That had been a rather dramatic turn of events. She knew his father had died recently, and it had been tactless of her to use it as part of her argument. But what other choice did she have? The most lucrative wedding contract of her career was within touching distance and she had personally promised the bride Castello Bellamo. If she failed to deliver she could say goodbye to her miraculous gateway into society weddings. Her name would be worthless.

She was not going to be ruined without a fight.

Leo slid in behind the bar of the empty upper mezzanine of the club and waved off the young barmaid with an impatient hand. Taking down a bottle of aged whisky, he poured himself a generous glass and let the amber liquid burn down his throat in one fluid movement.

Blondie had caught him by surprise—there was no doubting that. Beautiful women were not a rarity in his world—supermodels and socialites lined up to be seen on his arm—but there had been something about that determined grey gaze that had sparked his interest in a way no woman had for months now.

No one had dared speak to him of his father since his death had been worldwide news. But to start with that and then make a move for the castle… He took another swig of whisky, a harsh bark of laughter escaping his throat. She definitely had nerve—he'd give her that.

As his temper slowly calmed he realised he was no longer alone in the private bar. Miss Devlin had come to a stop on the other side of the counter.

'Just so we're clear: I am not a messenger and I don't play games. Ever.'

She was angry, and it was a sight to behold.

'Never? You keep shattering my fantasies tonight, Miss Devlin.' Leo took in the crisp white shirt she wore, the outline of a lacy white bra barely visible at the front. His knuckles tensed on the glass in his hand as heat rushed through his veins. Damn, it had been way too long if the sight of a bra was arousing him.

'Do you take anything seriously, Mr Valente?'

She rolled her eyes, checking the time on her watch in a gesture of boredom. But Leo could see the hint of a flush high on her cheekbones. She wasn't as unaffected by him as she pretended to be.

He stepped forward, bracing his hands

on the bar between them. 'Believe me, there are certain things I can take *very* seriously.' He let his eyes linger on her lips for a moment and smiled when she self-consciously took a step back. 'Look around you, Miss Devlin. I opened this club ten years ago. I now own one in every major city in the world, so you can see that I take the business of pleasure very seriously.'

'I'm here to talk about my proposal—not about pleasure.' She shook her head.

'A pity. I can tell that we would communicate very well on that subject.' He watched as heat flushed across her chest.

She laid her bag down forcefully on the counter. 'Are you always this forward?' Her voice was somehow calm and furious at the same time.

Damn it, but she was right. He was behaving like a caveman. What was it about this woman that set his teeth on edge? She was prickly, and direct, and sexy as hell. But she was here to talk about the one thing he was determined to ignore.

'You seem to have caught me off guard. Having an unarmed woman bypass a million-euro security system will do that to a man.'

'If I were a man would you be any less impressed, I wonder?' She stood tall, meeting his gaze evenly.

Leo laughed, offering her a glass of whisky. 'You are refreshing, Dara. Consider this a peace offering for my inappropriate behaviour.'

'Thank you.'

She took the glass with both hands, holding it close to breathe in the aroma. It was a ridiculously feminine gesture.

Leo watched her for a moment, downing the rest of his drink in one go. 'You know, considering your position, I wonder how *I* have come to be the one apologising.'

'I can be very persuasive.' She smiled and took a sip of whisky, making a delicate little hum of approval.

Leo felt his blood pump a little faster. 'Something we both have in common.'

He stepped out from behind the bar, taking in her polite business suit once more. She was a walking contradiction, this one. All delicate and businesslike on the outside, but with the guts to scale a building in a skirt and heels. He wondered why he hadn't thrown her out yet.

She placed her glass down, turning to face him head-on with calm determination in the set of her shoulders. 'I will be leaving for Sicily in the morning. I'm asking you please to just consider my proposal.'

'You just broke the law and you expect me to do business with you?'

'I am asking you to at least give me a chance.' Her voice remained steady, with not a trace of remorse for tonight's actions.

'Do you honestly expect me to let you use a seven-hundred-year-old castle for a glorified circus?'

'Firstly, it's a wedding. Secondly, from what I understand the castle has been mostly unoccupied for years. Many jobs were lost when your father closed it to the public. We both know that poverty is already an issue in Sicily.'

'I think you overestimate my ability to empathise.' He had heard the same argument before countless times.

'Maybe so, but a high-profile wedding

like this would bring a lot of opportunity to a struggling town like Monterocca.'

Leo felt the skin behind his neck prickle at her mention of the name. There was no reason for him to feel anything for that place. The people of his home town meant nothing to him. And yet he felt an uncomfortable pull in his stomach at her words.

'It would bring a storm of paparazzi,' he countered.

'Naturally. But from what I hear that might not be such a bad thing.'

He raised a brow in surprise. 'Have you been reading the tabloids, Dara?'

'I have been told that you have something of a bad reputation among the people of Sicily.'

'My father's reputation. Not mine,' he corrected.

'Yes, but his reputation has stood in your way in the past. It doesn't go unnoticed that you don't own a single club in your native region.'

Leo fought the urge to snarl. That was a particular sore spot of his. Opting instead for a nonchalant shrug of his shoulder, he leaned in. 'If I didn't know better, I'd say you cared.'

She straightened immediately, her guard firmly in place. 'Thankfully we both know that caring isn't high on the agenda here.' She gestured to the empty tables around them. 'So, this is the big exclusive launch party?'

'It's just a pre-launch. The lower floors are open to a select few guests. Tomorrow is the official event.' Leo looked down to where the floor below was filled with a swarm of people.

She followed him over to the floor-to-ceiling window that overlooked the entire club.

'Do you only mingle with the little people at official events?' she asked.

'Well, I have been kept busy up here by a very persistent blonde security breach, it seems.'

She ignored that comment, her delicate features taking on a focused edge. 'Did you know that those water features are blocking off the lounge area from the rest of the club?' she asked.

Leo blinked, following her gaze to take in the scene below them.

She continued. 'Also, the spotlights are a little too strong on the dance floor. Softer red-hued lighting would soften the transition into the seated areas.'

He followed her gaze with interest. 'Is there anything else you'd like to point out?'

She opened her mouth briefly, then stopped as if rethinking her actions.

'Oh come now, you've already begun—don't hold back on my account.' He raised a brow in challenge, noting the delicate glow on her cheekbones as she nipped at the skin of her lower lip.

'It's just…your staff's uniforms. They don't fit the image at all. They're quite… sparkly and frivolous.'

'Platinum is the signature colour,' he argued. 'They don't *sparkle*—they shine.'

She shrugged. 'They look sparkly to me. I wasn't trying to insult your style.'

'I thought you were all about honesty?' he scolded, frowning.

'I'm just trying to prove to you that I know what I'm talking about. No matter what kind of event you're throwing, the principle is always the same. Make it memorable, and make a statement. You're dealing with an exclusive clientele here—people who expect one-of-a-kind events every time. And that just happens to be my area of expertise.'

'You could see all of that from up here?'

'I have a keen eye for detail. I may not be the star guest of the party, but I make it my business to know how to plan one.'

'And my club does not fit your usual standard?'

'I don't have a "usual standard". In my world there is perfection or failure.'

'Ah, so this would be a failure?' He waited patiently for her answer.

Dara remained silent.

He let out a low bark of laughter. 'I've honestly never had someone insult me in order to convince me to sign a contract.'

'I believe in honesty. And if you choose Devlin Events to represent the *castello*, honesty is what you will get.'

He looked down at the crowd for a moment. 'So your plan is to throw a fancy wedding and fix my public image all in one go, is it? I'd say you're a little out of your league.'

'My résumé speaks for itself. I've personally forged contracts with some of the major resort chains around the island—Santo, Lucchesi and Ottanta.'

'You've worked for the Lucchesi Group?'

'I'm a freelance consultant. They hired me on a few occasions. The most notable being Umberto and Gloria's golden wedding anniversary. It was just a small garden party at their family home, but—'

Leo's business mind perked up at that. 'You are on first-name terms with Umberto Lucchesi?'

'Yes. He did offer me a job, which I politely refused. I prefer to be my own boss.'

Leo walked to the glass wall and looked down across the packed club below the mezzanine. Well, this had just gone from interesting to downright serendipitous. He wondered if she realised the significance of what she had just divulged. Maybe it was all a fabrication—she had researched him, after all.

But he knew there was no record of his history with Lucchesi…their recent disagreements. Business was a private affair among Sicilian men, and while he hadn't set foot on Sicilian soil in more than eighteen years he was still *siciliano* through and through.

He cursed as his phone rang, and the call took less than ten seconds before he ended it.

'I'm needed downstairs. Certain guests are getting impatient.'

Her eyes fell, and defeat was evident in the droop of her shoulders. 'Well, thank you for your time, Mr Valente.' She held her hand out to him.

He ignored it. 'It's Leo. And you misunderstand me. This conversation isn't over.'

'It's not?'

'Not by a long shot.' He smiled. 'One hour. We'll discuss this further then.'

She moved uneasily. 'Shall I stay up here?'

'You deserve to relax after your little stunt tonight, Dara. Come down to the dark side—drink, dance. Practise using the stairs, perhaps.' He began walking away, back towards his private elevator.

'But how will I know where to meet you?' she called.

'Don't worry. I'll find you.'

Leo smiled to himself as the elevator doors closed slowly, her shapely silhouette disappearing from view. He would finish this interesting interlude, and that was a promise.

CHAPTER TWO

LEATHER BARSTOOLS REALLY were a girl's worst enemy.

Dara sighed and adjusted the hem of her pencil skirt for what felt like the hundredth time. Glamorous socialites and powerful businessmen lined the dance floor, each designer dress more chic than the last. She felt hopelessly mismatched in her black skirt suit. She tapped the email app on her phone, even though it had barely been five minutes since the last check.

With a dull flicker, her emails vanished before her eyes. The screen turned completely blank.

Of course—a dead battery. She stuffed the useless device back into her bag. Was there anything that hadn't gone wrong tonight?

She was not an impatient person, but the music in here was too loud and it was about a million degrees too warm. Add that to the fact that an extremely rude group of models had commented on her appearance the moment she'd sat down. Her designer suit might as well have been rags next to their glamorous cocktail dresses.

At events like this she was the one who usually stood on the sidelines, barking into her headset at her team. Sitting idly at a bar just made her feel on edge.

Out of habit she scanned the room, noticing details about the layout and decor. For such an elite event, the organisation was nowhere near as fine-tuned as she would expect. And, as she'd told Leo Valente, the staff's uniforms were nothing short of theatrical—gauche, shiny silver tunics intended to represent the brand name: Platinum.

The sooner she wrapped up this meeting, the better. She was restless when she wasn't doing something productive. Winter was low season, mostly taken up with administrative tasks. She already missed the hectic schedule of her summer wedding list.

She huffed out an agitated breath and craned her neck to scan the crowd for the object of her thoughts once more. Her stomach lurched as she spotted him.

He stood on the opposite side of the dance floor, surrounded by members of the media. From her vantage point she could see that he stood head and shoulders above the other men, his broad shoulders fitting his tailored suit jacket to perfection.

She shouldn't be noticing his shoulders. She should be furious that he seemed to have forgotten about his promise. That 'one hour' had been up twenty minutes ago.

She fanned herself with a beer mat and looked up just in time to see a silver-clad bartender place an elaborate drink in front of her.

'Sorry, I didn't order this.' She pushed it slowly back towards him, only for him to slide it right back.

'Compliments of Signor Valente. For his beautiful blonde companion.' He smiled politely.

Apparently he hadn't forgotten her after all, she thought. Maybe this was his apology for leaving her waiting? She stared at the drink. It was a frothy cream-coloured cocktail that smelled of rich liqueur.

'What is it?' she asked as she took a small sip.

The young bartender smirked, leaning in closer. 'I believe in English it is called a Screaming Orgasm.'

A screaming *what*?

Her breath fought with an unfortunate sip of the offending cocktail, making her splutter her outrage noisily onto the counter.

Dara felt her face turn bright red. The bartender moved away, but not before she caught a glimpse of him laughing to himself. Of all the most blatant disregards for propriety, this was just outrageous.

She looked around and sure enough the group of models were now eyeing her even more intently. One of them commented loudly that clearly Valente's standards must be dropping.

Dara felt her cheeks burn with embarrassment. Was this why he'd asked her to stay here? Did Leo Valente expect her to sleep with him in order to get her contract? The thought sent a shiver of something suspiciously close to excitement down her spine.

She shook the foreign sensation off with a frown. She needed his help—that was true. But not at the expense of her pride. She had been a fool to promise Castello Bellamo to Portia Palmer without researching its owner first. Her choice was to sit here and act as a billionaire's plaything for the night or leave and face the consequences.

Her business reputation might be salvaged, but her pride...that was another matter entirely.

Making her decision, she grabbed her bag and pushed her way through the crowd towards the exit. Her heels ached with each step and the music seemed to be getting louder and louder. When she finally emerged out into the cool night air she felt as if she had just escaped hell itself.

Damn Leo Valente and his perfect unobtainable castle. Standing out in the chilly October air, she remembered that her phone was dead. She stalked her way back towards the club and asked the hostess to call her a cab. The dark-haired woman looked as if she might refuse for a moment, but thankfully nodded and disappeared inside.

Dara stood at the edge of the pavement and hugged her blazer tighter around her shoulders. Was she overreacting here? Maybe she should go back inside and give it one last try. The alternative was admitting to Portia Palmer that she had lied about being able to make her dream wedding in Monterocca a reality. The actress famously blacklisted anyone who got on her bad side.

Promising a location that everyone had tried to get for years and then taking it away most definitely qualified as bad.

She didn't know what on earth had possessed her to make such a ridiculous claim. She usually played by the rules, and she always came out on top. Why couldn't she have got landed with a kindly old man to convince rather than a hot-blooded Sicilian with a cruel sense of humour?

The door of the club slammed and jolted her out of her reverie. Dara spun round and came face-to-face with the object of her thoughts.

'Do you always run away from business meetings or am I just an exception?' he said, coming to a stop in front of her on the pavement. He was breathing heavily, as though he had just run through the entire club.

'I would hardly call being sat at a bar and plied with obscenely named alcohol a business meeting.' She folded her arms across her chest.

'You looked like you needed to laugh. Perhaps it was in bad taste.' He shrugged.

'You really do have a twisted sense of humour.' Dara huffed out a breath. 'I'm not prepared to…to play any games in order to get what I want here.'

He raised a brow, obviously understanding her meaning. 'Sorry to disappoint, but I'm not in the habit of coercing women into my bed.'

Dara's cheeks burned with embarrassment. 'Either way, I would be waiting until hell freezes over for you to hire out your castle. You practically said it yourself.'

'Castello Bellamo is my bargaining chip. Prove yourself to me and I will consider the contract.'

'Prove myself to you *how*, exactly?'

'The grand launch event tomorrow night will be very high profile. You seem to have a lot of opinions—I'd like to see you in action.'

Dara frowned. 'I don't understand…are you trying to offer me a job?'

'I'm offering you an audition to convince me of why I should trust you. A temporary consulting position, of sorts. Impress me and I'll go through your proposal. It's more than anyone else has ever gotten.'

She ignored the silky tone in his voice. 'But why offer me a chance in the first place? What's your game?'

He made a clucking sound. 'So untrusting, Dara. I'm curious to see if you're as ruthlessly ambitious as you say you are.'

'So if I pass the test, then you'll trust me?'

'Perhaps… But what kind of a businessman would I be if I trusted every beautiful blonde who offered me a deal?' He extended a hand towards her. 'So, Dara Devlin, are you prepared to risk your perfect reputation for a crumbling old castle?'

'"Risk" implies that I stand to fail.'

She accepted his hand and felt a frisson of electricity as his gaze intensified. The heat of his body seemed to flow up her veins. All of a sudden he was closer, his scent bombarding her senses as he leaned his body towards her. He pressed his lips to one cheek, then slowly progressed to the other.

Dara stood frozen as he eased back from her. The kiss was customary—she had got used to the gesture soon after moving to this country—but being so close to him, feeling the heat from his body scant inches from hers... She cleared the surprise from her expression, finding him watching her closely.

'My driver will see that you get back to your hotel safely.' He gestured to the town car that had pulled up by them. 'Until tomorrow, Dara...'

One last look and he was gone, walking back into his den of sin.

Dara watched him go, the realisation of what she had just agreed to making her insides flutter. She had just got further with Castello Bellamo than anyone had ever come before. But she felt as though she had calmly agreed to swim in a tank full of hungry sharks. No, she corrected herself, not sharks plural. One shark in particular.

Leo Valente was a smooth-talking predator, and she had somehow managed to catch his interest. She wouldn't let this chance go to waste. First she would wow him with her event expertise—then present him with her proposal for the castle. She smiled as she thought of his arrogant confidence. Sometimes even sharks needed to be taught a lesson.

Dara's hotel wasn't particularly fancy, but for such short notice it was good value and it didn't have bugs in the beds. That was good enough for her.

She decided to take the stairs down to the lobby to use up some of the nervous energy she had accumulated since leaving the club last night. After lying awake since dawn, staring into the distance, she had sprung out of bed and begun typing some ideas she'd had for the event tonight. They were good ideas—maybe some were even great—but that didn't mean they would be heard. After getting dressed and pacing the room for an hour, she'd decided against it.

Whatever Leo Valente's plan was for her this evening, she doubted it had anything to do with her organisation skills. It was up to her to convince him to contract Castello Bellamo out to her by not giving him a chance to ignore her logic.

She decided that she might as well see the sights while she mentally tortured herself. Whatever it was that he had in store for her, she was going to give it her all.

The lobby of the hotel had a small tourist kiosk. She approached the guide behind the counter and asked for some basic tools to see the main sights of Milan in a few short hours. The girl quickly began gathering various maps and brochures for her to plan her journey. She would need tickets for the trams, she announced, and headed through a small door behind the desk.

Dara picked up an Italian tabloid magazine and began carelessly flipping through the pages while she waited. Her hands stopped on an image of a familiar tall, dark Sicilian nightclub owner on a page entitled 'The Lonely Hearts Club'.

Dara almost laughed at the thought of Leo Valente being lonely. The man had women falling at his feet wherever he went. In this particular candid shot he was pictured bare-chested, sitting by a pool, and the look on his face was one of absolute boredom rather than lovesickness. The small bubble printed next to his head indicated that 'poor Leo' was tired of a life of supermodel flings and was ready to settle down. *'Is there a lioness brave enough to tame him?'* the final line wondered.

She turned to the next page, refusing to look at him. A lion indeed—that suited him much better than a shark. She had read somewhere before that lions liked to play with their food before they ate it. If ever there was an apt description for Leo Valente, that was it.

Her mind flashed back to the way he had looked at her last night, and she ignored the shiver of awareness that coursed through her. Sure, he was an attractive man—she could hardly deny that. But she had spent the past five years ignoring countless attractive men and she wouldn't be stopping now. Her career plan didn't leave time for men, and she was quite happy to keep it that way.

'Brushing up on current events, Dara?'

She snapped up her head in surprise, only to be pinned by a familiar smirking emerald gaze.

Leo raised a brow in silent question. 'My "lonely heart" is apparently worthy of your attention this morning... I didn't take you as the type to read gossip.'

Dara looked down and realised she was still holding the trashy magazine. 'I don't.' She said it a little too quickly. 'I'm just browsing while I wait for some travel information.'

She shoved the offending publication

hastily back into the stand, straightening up to push an errant tendril of hair behind her ear.

He seemed taller and more imposing than he had the night before, if that was even possible. Dark jeans and a brown leather jacket accentuated the rough casual air that seemed to surround him wherever he went.

How had he known she was staying here? She didn't remember mentioning the name of her hotel to him. And besides, his event wasn't scheduled for another eight hours. Was he here to tell her he had decided not to give her a chance after all? Last night she had been lucky. She had caught him off guard, piqued his interest. Maybe he had woken up this morning and realised that this was one impulse he could erase.

She reflected on her black skinny jeans and warm woollen sweater, wishing she had worn something more professional. She had decided to be sensible today, choosing flat patent pumps for her plan of walking around the city. Now, as he stood in front of her, she felt short for the first time in her life. She was tall at five foot eight—especially by Italian standards. But she barely reached his chin.

Just then the kiosk attendant returned from behind the counter and placed a small tram card on the counter next to her bundle of maps and brochures.

'She doesn't need these any more.' Leo pushed the items back towards the attendant with a polite nod. The poor girl was clearly starstruck, with her head bobbing up and down and two bright pink spots on either cheek.

Dara groaned. Was that what she had looked like last night? She needed to remind herself to think sad thoughts when her painfully pale Irish skin decided to play up.

'I was planning to use those.' She reached towards the documents on the counter. She didn't care who he was—she wasn't going to let him hijack her day on another of his whims.

'The last time I checked you were *mine* for today.' His eyes glittered as he leaned casually on the counter. 'Like you said last night, Dara, I'm an impulsive man. If you want to work with me so badly, you need to learn to live by my rules. If I decide to take you to lunch, you drop your plans.'

Dara felt a shiver run down the back of her neck. This was ridiculous. He was practically ordering her to obey. She tried to think of a witty retort—something to wipe away that confident lift of his brow. Nothing came. She was here to audition for a role, and therefore she had to play his game. If that meant dropping her plans at his request, then so be it.

'Consider them dropped.' She fitted her bag under her arm and tilted her chin in what she hoped was a confident expression. 'I'm entirely at your disposal.'

One corner of his mouth tilted upwards, 'Congratulations. You just passed the first test. But I don't intend to dispose of you, Dara—not just yet.'

Leo had never thought he would get such satisfaction in seeing a woman eat. The rooftop *trattoria* was a little gem he liked to visit when he was in Milan, but he couldn't remember ever being so transfixed by a female companion before. She ate so carefully, spinning each forkful of spaghetti until it was wound tight before sliding it into her mouth. She refused to speak with a full mouth, and looked positively horrified when he did so without thought.

She had chosen spaghetti with fresh mixed seafood after enquiring about the specialities. She hadn't asked for a menu, and had graciously accepted the waiter's recommendations for a mixed appetiser platter they could share. The silver-haired Tuscan had positively beamed with delight at her accent when she spoke. Such a polite blonde foreigner with a clear Sicilian dialect—she was quite the novelty.

He took a sip of his sparkling water, watching as she placed the last forkful into her mouth. She had been eating so delicately he had hardly noticed that she had demolished the entire dish.

'Food is another passion of yours, I see.' He smiled.

She dabbed the napkin lightly at her mouth. 'Since I moved here—definitely.'

He followed the neat little movement

of her hands as she placed her fork across the plate. The waiter promptly came and cleared the table, offering them an array of desserts which they both politely declined.

She sighed and sat back unselfconsciously in her seat, satisfied by the large meal. He imagined that might be how she looked after other types of satisfaction, and his stomach clenched at the thought.

Distracting himself, he stirred sugar into his coffee. 'A woman who likes to eat is a rarity in my world.'

She turned her head to look out of the window, across the dull Milanese skyline. 'The women in your world must be very sad and hungry.'

Leo smiled. 'The *siciliani* must have thought they were dreaming to find such a beautiful woman in their company who finishes a full meal.' He took a sip of the coffee, feeling the familiar strength hit his tastebuds.

She ignored his compliment. 'Actually, when I first moved to Syracuse all I ate were ham sandwiches and spaghetti in tomato sauce.'

'That's punishable by law in this country,' he scolded.

She smiled, nodding her head. 'I found that out soon enough. I think I lasted about a week before a colleague dragged me to her grandmother's house and made me confess my crimes.'

'Italian grandmothers are not known to be forgiving—especially when it involves food. I'm surprised you survived.'

Leo thought of his own upbringing. The array of servants in the castle kitchen. The silent meals alone with his nanny. Surprising himself with the direction of his thoughts, he sat forward, focusing on Dara's smiling features.

'It wasn't a laughing matter. That woman cooked twelve different types of pasta in the space of one hour.' She shook her head. 'It was the most dramatic reaction to food I have ever encountered.'

'My countrymen are not known for their delicate sensibilities.' He finished his coffee, regarding her as she sat still looking pensively out of the window. 'Tell the truth:

have you eaten a plain tomato sauce since then?'

That earned him a smile. 'Not if my life depended on it.'

'Then you've passed the second test,' he proclaimed.

He watched as her expression drifted, all trace of their playful conversation melting away.

'Exactly how many tests do you have in store for me?' she asked as she took a sip from her water.

He leaned back into his seat, casual and in control. 'I don't like to put a limit on progress, Dara. As a businesswoman I'm sure you can understand that.'

'I'm glad to hear that, actually. I was considering showing you some ideas that struck me for your event tonight.' She reached for her handbag, then paused. 'Unless that violates my role as your temporary consultant?' She raised a brow.

Leo sighed. The woman was hell-bent on annoying him.

'Make it quick.'

She busied herself taking out a sleek tablet computer and unfolding the case into a neat stand, so that it stood upright as an impromptu presentation screen. She launched into a flurry of rough outlines, pinpointing the areas in which she felt his current plan lacked variety.

'So, you see, if you split the evening into two parts you will avoid alienating the business clientele,' she concluded, finally.

Leo sat back in his chair and tilted his head to one side. The flow chart on the screen was genius. She had just achieved in one brainstorming session what a team of seven event organisers had failed to.

The Milan relaunch had been heavily debated for weeks, due to the awkward combination of 'party hard' celebrity guests and the more staid businessmen and politicians. Finding an event structure that could keep all groups entertained had proved impossible, and yet Dara had seen the solution after simply looking down from an upper floor window.

'Could you achieve all of this before you attend the event tonight?'

'Without a doubt.' She nodded confidently, her grey eyes lighting up with determination.

'I'll call my team in and you can get to work.'

She looked surprised for a moment. 'Would your team not resent having a newcomer treading on their toes?'

'I'm beginning to wonder if *I* should be the one resenting them.'

She visibly relaxed into her chair. 'I'm glad you're open to change.'

He laughed, taking a sip of his coffee. '"Change" is an understatement. Things clearly need a shake-up. They're paid so well they've lost their creativity.' He sat forward, flicking the screen of her computer across to look through the images once more. 'I'll have my management team on hand—anything you need, they are at your disposal.'

'You make me sound important.' Her eyes sparkled as she closed down the screen and placed it back into her bag.

'And what about the uniforms?' he enquired casually, and smiled when her expression turned rueful.

'I don't expect you to overhaul your branding after one little statement.'

'Ah, but I'm an impulsive man, Dara.' He waved a hand, signalling to the waiter for their coats. 'Your comments last night have wounded my overblown pride. I'll expect that to be remedied by this evening too.'

Her eyes widened, her delicate hands twisting in her lap as she absorbed his challenge. 'It take it that this is another test?'

'You say you've never lost a challenge. Consider it an experiment.'

She straightened her shoulders. 'You trust me to make changes to your event *and* overhaul your signature uniform in less than seven hours?'

'Are you telling me you can't do it?'

'I can do it,' she said, all confidence. 'I just don't understand why you're giving me this opportunity when you've refused so many others.'

He sat back in his chair, once again taken by her honest approach to business. He had invited her tonight because of his attraction to her. But now, after she had once again proved she was more brains than body, he felt tempted to tell her at least a half-truth.

'Ten years ago I commissioned those uniforms as a gimmick. We had only been open a few months, and it was the first New Year's Eve event we ever held. The party was in full swing when a notorious designer came staggering in. He was drunk, as usual, and he stood in the middle of a crowd of journalists and began to shout that he could see himself in one of the suits.'

Leo laughed as he remembered the night clearly.

'The man was absolutely trashed, and he was amazed by his own reflection in the material.' He rolled his eyes. 'But that's not how everyone else saw it. Anyway— long story short: word soon spread and our temporary costumes became a brand statement. I found the whole situation hilarious.'

He took another sip of coffee.

'It was a publicity stunt that worked, and it seemed that I was the only person who could see how ridiculous the staff looked. Until you, of course.' He raised his coffee cup in mock salute.

'My attention to detail is what keeps me in business.'

'Well, I'd imagine being associated with a big brand like Lucchesi doesn't hurt.' Leo dropped the name casually, watching her reaction with hooded intent.

'I'm hardly "associated" with the brand. I've been contracted for a few events—one with the Lucchesi Foundation, their charity for the hospitals of Sicily.'

'You must have made quite an impression for a relative unknown to be trusted by such a family.'

'I happened to get talking to Gloria Lucchesi and her daughters while I was planning a wedding in Syracuse.' She shrugged. 'I wish it was more impressive, but it was rather coincidental.'

'Nonetheless, you are on first-name terms with a very powerful family. That in itself is an achievement.'

'I suppose it is.' She smiled.

Leo mulled over her connection to Umberto Lucchesi. Their recent disagreement had caused a large problem that he was fast losing time to resolve. Not that a wedding planner could pose any solution, but she might possibly be useful.

He watched as Dara sat back in her chair, casually glancing towards him as she folded her napkin into a neat square on the table, then did the same with his.

She looked up and noticed his look of amusement at her actions. 'Sorry, it's a force of habit. Organisation is a natural impulse for me. Hence my choice of occupation.'

'And what does my choice of occupation say about me, I wonder?'

She twisted her lips. 'I don't think it would be appropriate for me to say.'

'You know, not very many women can make me feel as if I'm under scrutiny. And yet it's as though everything I say or do offends you.'

'I'm not offended by you. I'm quite aware of the fact that your impulses are the only reason I'm sitting here.' She shrugged.

'Oh, I wouldn't say that's the only reason…' He let his voice deepen slightly as he leaned forward and met her eyes. Dark blonde eyelashes lowered for one split second and her pupils dilated, leaving only a rim of steel grey around them.

That one reflex was enough to tell him what he'd come here to find out. No matter how indifferent she claimed to be, she most definitely was not unaffected by this intense chemistry between them.

'You are here because I want you to be. I always get what I want.'

He smiled as her eyes darkened even more, but this time in anger. Oh, yes, she was just what he needed to break his little spell of restlessness. He would break down each of those polite little barriers one by one, until she couldn't think straight any more.

She responded by throwing him her most polite smile. 'I understand that you're a powerful man, Leo, and that you grew up in a certain way. But sooner or later you will find that not everyone bends to your will. No matter how much you push.'

He ignored her comment about his privileged past. He was used to people's ignorant presumptions. He most definitely *had* grown up a certain way—but not the way most people would expect.

He leaned across the table, raising one brow in challenge. 'Are you sure about that? I've been known to be quite persuasive.'

'Well, there's something we have in common.' She smiled, and for a second he caught a glimpse of the fire buried underneath all that ice. He was enjoying sitting here with her, enjoying their sparring. She was nothing like any woman who had sparked his interest before.

She stood up as the waiter approached with their items from the cloakroom. 'I came here with one goal, Leo. And I never find myself off track—no matter how distracting the scenery.'

'I would expect nothing less.' He nodded in agreement.

She paused. 'Good. Because I won't be playing any more of your games. I'm a professional, and I like to get things done quickly.'

'As do I, Dara,' he purred.

Always the gentleman, he held out her coat, helping her to fit it comfortably around her shoulders. One errant finger lightly grazed the sensitive skin of her neck and he felt her shiver in response. Smiling, he eased back as she turned to face him.

'*Allora*, I think we understand each other,' he said, shrugging on his own coat quickly.

She continued to watch him with a mixture of accusation and reluctant awareness as they made their way outside into the chilly autumn afternoon. He stopped when his chauffeur approached them, opening the door of the limo with polite efficiency.

'My driver will take you to the club. My team will be at your command.'

Leo fought the urge to slide in beside her on the seat. She felt every ounce of this tension between them—he had seen it in her eyes. She wanted him, but she wouldn't let herself have what she wanted. That was a lesson that only came after prolonged temptation. He would show her just what it meant to lose control—but first he'd have to take her out of that comfort zone of hers.

CHAPTER THREE

DARA STOOD ON the lower floor of the club and made a final sweep of her surroundings. Leo's team had been very responsive to her advice—in fact they'd seemed almost relieved to have the responsibility taken from their shoulders. None of them had seemed particularly overjoyed to be planning such a high-profile event. Maybe Leo was right: they were jaded by success and lacked any motivation to strive further.

Well, that suited her just fine. Being in close proximity to such high-profile guests was a networking dream come true. She would make a few new contacts, get her own event contract signed, and then fly straight home to set about planning the wedding of her career. Finally her strict business plan was yielding the kind of results she had dreamed of when she'd left her life in Dublin behind.

Unconsciously she chewed on her bottom lip, trying to supress the memories that her mind conjured up every time she thought of her past life. The well-meaning glances filled with pity…the hushed conversations. She would forever be known as poor Dara Devlin back home—it had been the main reason she left it all behind. It would have been impossible to forge a new life in a place filled with such painful memories.

She remembered sitting in the hospital, her dream of ever having a child having just been taken away from her. Only to find herself watching her fiancé coldly walk away from her for the last time.

No. She shook off the thoughts before they could take hold. She had done enough wallowing in the weeks before she had decided to move to Italy. Her life was good now. She should thank Daniel, really. He had set her free to focus on what she really loved. Her career gave her more satisfaction than family life ever could have. She was happy now—she truly was—and now she had the chance to *really* make a name for herself.

Portia Palmer was the biggest movie star Ireland had produced in the past ten years, and she had chosen Dara to plan her huge weekend wedding. She liked to think that the actress had somehow heard a glowing report from one of her happy clients. But sadly it most likely had more to do with Dara being the only Irish planner on the island. Miss Palmer was all about patriotism and her Celtic heritage.

But that was fine with Dara. Publicity was publicity, and if she hoped for her name to gain status it couldn't hurt to have a world-famous Hollywood star in her little black book.

Now, after seeing tonight's guest list, she felt butterflies flapping around in her stomach with nerves and anticipation. Leo hadn't been lying when he'd said he had high-profile guests. One quick flip through the hostess's list had revealed several notable European politicians, at least three racing drivers, a world-renowned fashion designer and the entire cast of the Luscious

Lingerie catalogue. People like that could open more than doors for her in her career. They could knock down walls.

The snooty hostess from the night before suddenly appeared by her side. Dara closed the list with a snap, trying not to look guilty.

'Signor Valente has instructed me to give you this.' The woman sniffed, holding out a small business card. She seemed quite unimpressed to be running such lowly errands for her employer.

Dara took the card with muttered thanks. It was plain black, with the single line of an address printed on the front. Nothing to indicate what kind of business it was.

'Am I supposed to go there?' she asked quickly as the hostess began to walk away. 'Did he not tell you anything else?'

The woman turned back and shrugged one shoulder, thoroughly bored with the conversation. 'I am told to give you this and make sure you go to the address.'

The event was less than two hours away, so Dara wasted no time in grabbing her things and taking the sleek chauffeur-driven town car that Leo had provided. Whatever this errand was, she needed to get back to her hotel soon if she stood a chance of looking half decent.

The car came to a smooth stop on one of the most upmarket streets in Milan. Giants of Italian fashion stood shoulder to shoulder here, with shopfronts that screamed luxury. But the address on the black card led her down a narrow alleyway to a door of exactly the same deep, nondescript black.

Her hand was hovering uncertainly over the knocker when the door swung open to reveal a tall fair-haired man in a sleek pin-striped suit.

'*Mademoiselle*, we've been waiting for you,' he said, taking her by the hand and leading her inside.

'Excuse me? I don't even know—'

He continued to lead her along by the hand, 'Just follow me.'

He was definitely French, she thought as they made their way up a short staircase to a large open-plan loft with carpet so white it hurt her eyes. The walls were mirrored on one side, and a few long purple drapes lined the wall on the other. Dara took a moment to look around, feeling hopelessly confused by the situation. Was she here to collect something?

'I was sent here by Leo Valente...' she began uncertainly. 'He didn't mention why—'

The blond man hushed her with a sudden snap of his fingers.

'We don't have time to chat. My team and I need to begin.'

As if on cue, a small army of women in black smocks appeared from behind one of the purple curtains. Dara caught a glimpse of row upon row of clothing racks before the curtain swung back into place, blocking her view.

'Hold on a minute—what *is* all of this?'

She raised a hand to stop the pinstripe-wearing bully as he loomed near, measuring tape in hand. A tight knot of tension formed in her stomach as one of the women hung a silky red dress on a hook beside the mirror.

The Frenchman gave an impatient sigh. 'We are here to style you, darling. Everything from hairpins to nail polish.' He glanced down at her short practical nails and frowned.

Dara clenched her fists, a mixture of embarrassment and anger forcing her to bite her lip. How dared that arrogant Sicilian brute organise this little stunt? As though she was some sort of pauper, here to be dressed up like one of the beautiful people for the night.

Indignation bubbled in her chest and she grabbed her phone from her handbag, ready to launch into a verbal attack on a certain nightclub mogul, only to realize that she didn't even have his phone number.

The memory of his face at lunchtime swam into her mind—that devilish smirk when she had shivered under his touch. He'd said he wasn't playing games any more, but that had been a lie. This little manoeuvre was designed to throw her off balance, to put him back in control. He clearly didn't like it that she was proving of practical use in tonight's event.

Willing herself to calm down, she took

a deep breath and looked back at the sultry red number mocking her from the corner of the room.

'Did Signor Valente choose this gown for me?' she asked in a deathly quiet whisper, watching with narrowed eyes as the blond man's bravado faltered.

'He picked it out himself this afternoon, *mademoiselle*.' He stood up straight to emphasise his point. 'It is one of a kind.'

Just like the man himself, she thought snidely. This was the same kind of stunt as the cocktail last night. No other man would be so obnoxious as to choose a gown for a woman he barely knew.

She walked across the room and ran her hand down the jewelled fabric. If Leo had sent her here to unsettle her...well, he had succeeded. The thought of wearing something so blatantly sexual was akin to tearing out her own fingernails. Dara did *not* do sexual—she didn't even do sex any more.

For the first time in five years she felt once again as if she wasn't good enough. As if she needed to change herself to fit the items on someone's list. And that just wouldn't do.

The blond man and his team of beauty assassins stood silently, watching her, hairbrushes and make-up wands like weapons in their utility belts.

She turned to face them, her eyes blazing with determination. 'I will be choosing something for myself.'

The Frenchman shook his head. 'Monsieur Valente has made his wishes very clear to my team.'

'Tell me, honestly, does this dress look like something I could pull off?' Dara gestured to the gown.

He turned his head to one side, examining her from head to toe with agonising intensity. 'Truthfully, no. Your chest is too flat to wear such a low neckline. And the colour is far too rich for such a pale complexion. Nonetheless, I refuse to go against my client's wishes.'

Dara ignored such blunt description of her flaws, crossing the room to stand in front of him, hands on her hips. 'Let's make one thing clear. *I* am your client. What will it do to your business if you send me out in such an ill-thought-out ensemble? It will be such a high-profile event too…'

She let her voice trail off and watched as his eyes widened with horror.

'I'm glad we understand each other.'

She smiled with satisfaction as he turned to his team and began barking orders to bring more dresses.

Leo looked at his watch as the guests started to filter in for the champagne hour. He was beginning to think that Little Miss Proper had decided to chicken out. His limo had gone to collect her over an hour ago. Taking another sip of the whisky he'd been nursing, he passed his gaze lazily around the room that Dara and his team had spent the afternoon finalising.

His coveted glass water features now sat in each corner of the dance floor. The overall effect made the room seem wider and brought much more attention to the features themselves. Low sofas flanked the dance floor, now an ideal space for the younger celebrity scene. The open area of the club was filled with loud pumping music, and the dance floor glowed with sultry lighting, giving it an almost mystical appearance.

In the entrance lounge a ten-foot champagne tower had been placed centre stage, and a clever little mechanism was sending glittering liquid down in an endless waterfall. The guests met at this feature and spread out easily, making the overall vibe sleek and relaxed. The upper lounge area had been transformed into a cocktail bar for the social elite crowd, its lower ceiling and distance from the dance floor making the noise less obtrusive and ideal for hushed business deals.

All in all, he was impressed.

He wasn't entirely sure what had compelled him to offer her this little audition—probably a mixture of curiosity and a mild attraction. Okay, so maybe *mild* wasn't the word for it…

He stood at the bar in the lower lounge, watching the guests arrive one by one. The night was just getting started but he was in no mood to play host.

Usually he would be the one in the middle of the crowd, with people hanging onto his every word. They would beg to hear about each of the once-in-a-lifetime adventures he'd been on. The wild parties, the daredevil stunts that the tabloids loved to cover. He had created an image for himself and his brand that drew people to him. But lately he had become steadily more jaded by the repetition in his lifestyle.

Until last night.

Dara had awoken a spark in him, and he felt the familiar hum of attraction driving him for the first time in months. Women had been far from his agenda while he dealt with the aftermath of his father's passing. His usually insatiable sexual appetite had been non-existent as he threw himself into his work.

He thought of how she might have reacted, seeing that red dress today. He knew she would be unprepared for such a high-glamour event, but admittedly his intentions were not entirely innocent. He was on edge, waiting for the inevitable explosion when she arrived. He was even considering making a phone call to his driver when a hand touched his shoulder.

Leo turned and immediately grasped the hand of the grey-haired man standing in front of him. 'Gianni—you got the invitation.'

'Well, I was hardly going to refuse a chance to see what else you've done to my club, boy,' he rasped.

Leo fought the urge to smile. His old friend hadn't changed one bit. Gianni Marcello was a dragon, but he was the closest thing to a father Leo ever had.

'The last time I checked this was still *my* club,' he corrected.

The old man waved a hand. 'A technicality. You smart-talked me into selling—just like you smart-talked your way to where you are now.' He paused to bark an order for two glasses of grappa at a startled waiter. 'You came to my hotel today. Since when did you start hand-delivering invitations?'

Leo smiled. 'I thought you might appreciate the gesture.'

Gianni snorted, unaffected. 'I was under

the impression that you had forgotten where I live after all this time.'

Leo shrugged one shoulder casually, but inside he felt hot shame creep up his neck. He'd known Gianni wouldn't make this reunion easy, but perhaps this wasn't the best of settings to hash out their differences. Leo contemplated walking away, under the pretext of having business responsibilities, but the old man knew him better than anyone.

Looking around the lounge, Gianni scoffed loudly. 'Do you have any damned chairs in this place, or do I have to build one myself?'

Leo laughed, leading the way up the mirrored steps to the upper lounge. He found them a quiet seat in the corner furthest from the crowd. A few business contacts from Paris sidetracked him, requiring the usual chit-chat before he could slide comfortably into the seat opposite Gianni at the low table.

Their drinks arrived promptly and Leo took a sip of the strong liquid, feeling it burn down his throat and warm his chest.

Gianni remained silent for a moment, watching him over the rim of his glass. The old man had always liked an air of suspense.

'You have made some powerful friends, I can see.' He gestured to a group of well-known city officials, sipping champagne down on the lower floor.

'A wise man once told me never to call a politician a friend,' Leo corrected.

Gianni nodded his head once. 'You always listened to me, boy.' He downed the rest of his drink in one go, setting it down harshly on the dark tempered glass. 'Except when it came to one thing.'

Leo sat back in his seat. He knew what was to come next. Had known the moment he'd decided to invite his old mentor. 'Go ahead and say what you came here to say. I owe you enough to listen this time.'

'Is that an apology for walking away from me six months ago?'

Leo averted his gaze, feeling like an unruly child being scolded for disobeying the rules. Gianni Marcello was the only man he had ever respected enough not to make jokes in a serious conversation.

'You should have come to the funeral.'

The accusation was quiet, and yet it hit Leo like a knife to the gut. He had known the words were coming, and yet he suddenly felt betrayed.

'I thought you above all people would understand.'

'I understand that you acted out of anger. And I taught you better than that.' Gianni sat forward across the table, dark eyes shrewd with accusation.

Leo felt his body tense until he was sure he would smash the glass in his hand. Willing himself to calm down, he took a deep breath and met the familiar eyes of the man he trusted with his deepest secrets. 'I assure you, Gianni, anger was the furthest thing from my mind. I made a decision not to pay empty respects to a man I hadn't seen or spoken to in years. I stopped losing my temper over my father a long time ago.'

'Is that why you sold off every share he left you?' Gianni spoke with deadly calm.

'Don't lie to me, boy. It was an act of cold-blooded revenge and we both know it.'

'He left me those shares hoping I'd be tempted to take my place as his rightful heir. He knew I'd never accept it.'

Gianni knew nothing of what his father was truly capable of. No one knew.

Gianni shook his head. 'I'm not telling you that you made the wrong decision. I'm saying that your motivation was out of character.'

Leo waited a moment before speaking. 'Did it disappoint you to find I am exactly like him after all?'

'If you were like him you wouldn't have walked away from an inheritance worth billions twelve years ago and then have the nerve to do it all again the first chance you got. Vittorio Valente would turn in his grave, knowing his entire corporation is in pieces.'

'My father made his choices and died with the consequences.'

Beautiful green eyes flashed into Leo's mind, along with a face filled with youth and vitality—his mother's face...a face he hadn't thought of in twelve years. He brushed it away, refusing to let the memory surface.

Gianni frowned. 'Don't let the memory of a ghost haunt you for ever. You are a good man, Leo, but you're heading down a lonely path.'

'Have you been reading those gossip magazines?' He chuckled. 'I'm perfectly content to work hard and play harder for the time being.' He leaned back in his seat, stretching his neck muscles in an effort to relieve the painful ache in his temples.

'I was married for thirty-five years. And look at me now. A lonely widower, living in my own hotel suites like a damned salesman.' Gianni took another slug of grappa, his eyes twinkling suspiciously. 'But my wife gave me three sons. A man should always have his own sons to carry on his legacy.'

'Some day, maybe.' Leo shrugged.

The thought of settling down wasn't unappealing. He just wasn't cut out for that kind of lifestyle. He could be needed anywhere around the world from one day to the next. He never stayed in one place long enough to set down roots. And besides, roots held you down, trapped you in one place. If there was one thing he couldn't stand it was feeling trapped.

He shook off the unwelcome thought, watching as Gianni visibly ogled a passing brunette.

'Maybe I should follow your lead and find myself some of those supermodels.' Gianni chuckled under his breath.

'Ah, they don't eat enough,' Leo jibed, and the sudden memory of Dara and her delicious lips as she ate stormed his thoughts.

'You never drank like a true Sicilian. Whisky is for Westerners.'

'You're still as politically incorrect as I remember.' Leo smiled.

The old man looked away for a moment. His expression was filled with sadness. 'You should have come to me, Leonardo. You always came to me.'

He looked confused, making him look every inch his seventy years. For the very first time Leo realised that the great dragon wasn't going to live for ever. The thought left an uncomfortable knot in his stomach.

He glanced across the lounge, wanting to end this conversation. Raking up the past did nothing for his temper.

A flurry of movement drew his eyes towards the edge of the lounge just as the loudest politician stopped speaking mid-sentence and pointed towards the tall blonde gracefully ascending the stairs.

She wasn't wearing the red dress. He almost wished she was. The dress he had chosen for her was deliberately risqué and playful—an attempt to take her out of her comfort zone. What she wore in its place was temptation personified.

A second skin of shimmering jewelled gold.

It fitted each curve so tightly it might as well have been painted on. He felt heat rush through his veins as he stood slowly, and their eyes met as she came to a stop by the bar. Raising one eyebrow, she made it clear he was going to have to come to her.

Gianni followed his gaze with interest.

'That one could freeze hell with those eyes. Finally you've found a real woman, eh?'

Leo heard Gianni chuckle loudly behind him, but he was already across the lounge in a few long strides.

She smiled sweetly as he came to a stop in front of her. 'My apologies for being late. It seemed to take quite a long time to make me look presentable.'

'You changed the dress.'

She tilted her head to one side. 'Is there something wrong with this one?'

He resisted the urge to run his gaze down her wicked curves again. The dress wasn't indecent, by any means, in fact by some standards it was almost modest. Small delicate sleeves stopped just at the shoulder and the neckline swooped gracefully along her collarbone. It was just that it hugged every delicious curve of her body—a body he was trying very hard to ignore at this moment.

'I decided your choice wasn't appropriate for this evening.'

She turned slightly and his throat went dry. The dress was sinfully low-cut at the back, leaving the graceful curve of her spine completely bare for everyone to see.

He coughed, clearing his throat. 'It wasn't a request, Dara. I thought you would understand that.'

Dara stepped closer, her voice lowered to a dangerous whisper. 'I'm confused. At any point during our meeting this afternoon did I indicate that I have difficulty in choosing my own clothing?' She raised one sleek blonde brow.

'You were unprepared for the formal dress code tonight. I was ensuring that you'd fit the part of my event planner.'

'Temporary consultant,' she corrected. 'Out of interest, do you ensure that all of your potential business partners have the opportunity to bare their cleavage?'

Leo floundered at that question. This was not going to plan at all.

Just then a familiar voice came from behind his left shoulder.

'Leonardo, are you going to introduce me to this beautiful creature?'

He turned to see Gianni, his watery brown eyes twinkling with amusement.

Leo closed his mouth and turned to the man, a playful glint in his eye. 'I was planning to keep her away from you as a matter of fact.'

'She looks like she's planning to keep away from you too.' He chuckled, extending a hand. 'Gianni Marcello. I don't think we've met.'

Dara stepped forward and politely introduced herself, all trace of hostility gone from her face.

'Dara is my event planner,' Leo explained casually.

'Actually, I'm just here for tonight,' she corrected, with a swift glance in his direction. 'Leo is in the process of negotiating with my company.'

'A businesswoman!' Gianni exclaimed, clapping his hands together with glee. 'Thank goodness he's found someone who can actually hold a conversation in company.'

Dara had opened her mouth to correct

him when they were suddenly interrupted by the club manager.

After a low murmured conversation with the man Leo turned back to them apologetically. 'It seems that it is time for the host to officiate,' he explained. 'Try not to bore her with your business talk.'

'He is quite the charmer, isn't he?'

Dara stopped watching Leo making his way across the floor below and turned to find the older man, Gianni, watching her with interest.

'I gave him his first job, you know. Tending bar in my flagship hotel in Paris. Now look at him—drinking champagne with supermodels.' He chuckled.

'You own the Marcello Hotel chain?'

'I do.' He smiled. 'But as far as work goes, my children do that now. I'm just enjoying my golden years in the town that made me.'

'Were you born here in Milan?' she asked.

'I was born and raised in Bella Sicilia.' He smiled again, eyes twinkling. 'Business brought me to the industrial north. I opened my first hotel here forty-five years ago.'

'The Grand Marcello Milan was your first?'

'She was my crowning glory. Hence the reason my apartment is on the top floor there.'

She smiled back. 'I love the branding of your chain. "New city, old friends".'

'That tagline is probably the only part of my original work that still lives on.' He tutted. 'Young people want to make everything modern.'

Dara nodded in agreement. The old man was nice. He had a cantankerous warmth about him that made her feel instantly comfortable.

The champagne hour was going well, she thought as she looked down across the crowd of Milan's glittering elite. All here to be photographed for the society pages, no doubt. Soon the lights would dim and the official event would fade into the background, allowing them to use the club for its true purpose. Privacy, anonymity and sin.

The music was lowered and a tinkling

sound resonated through the air. Dara looked down to see that Leo had moved up to the small stage erected in the middle of the dance floor. Gianni took her elbow and they made their way down to the lower floor as Leo began speaking.

He began to outline the concept of the club's renovation, explaining the fluid lines and mirrored backdrops. Gianni made a few more tutting noises beside her, commenting that it had been fine just the way it was.

Leo smiled brightly, ever the charismatic host, and he finished by thanking his team of staff in detail for their support.

'Finally, I have the greatest pleasure to introduce you all to a rising star in the industry—Miss Dara Devlin.'

To her horror he pointed her out in the crowd and she suddenly became the focus of three hundred curious stares.

What was he thinking? She was a nobody here. These people were looking at her as though expecting her to burst into song.

Leo smiled, oblivious to her horror. 'Miss Devlin is a recent discovery of mine, she is a rare creative talent in the industry. Such is her dedication to detail, she even gave the Platinum uniform a facelift to fit with our new theme.'

The crowd gave subdued applause, curious eyes glancing from the scarlet-faced event planner to the now very sleek waiters walking around all in black. Dara prayed for him to move on to another topic, breathing a sigh of relief when he began to wrap up the speech.

Gianni raised his brows beside her, seemingly quite entertained by the proceedings. 'He seems quite taken with you, *carina*.' He smiled.

Dara straightened her shoulders, trying in vain to dispel the heat from her cheeks. 'Mr Valente is a very successful man. I'm grateful to be working with him.' She took a sip from her cool soda water, feeling it hit her painfully dry throat.

'You are quite naive if you think he's just thinking about work.' His eyes twinkled.

Dara ignored the uncomfortable sensation in her stomach at his words. Leo *was* taking her seriously, now that she had proved her talent. There was a playful tension between them, of course, but she had no plans to act on it. Not at all.

She decided to ignore Gianni's comment, straightening her shoulders and saying, 'Actually, I'm negotiating an event contract for Castello Bellamo.'

The old man stilled, clearly taken by surprise with that information. Dara waited for him to speak, but he remained silent. Thinking it best to give him a moment, she looked out across the dance floor. Leo had just stepped down from the podium and began conversing with a group of men in sleek suits.

She looked down and saw that his eyes were trained on her even as he spoke. He was watching her intently, his green gaze seeming to reach across the dance floor to her. She should look away. She should restart her conversation with Gianni— something.

She turned back to see Gianni watching Leo with the most ferocious expression she had ever seen. 'Mr Marcello, is everything okay?' she asked tentatively.

'He's playing dangerous games. Excuse me for a moment.' His eyes darkened to furious points, and without another word the man began weaving forward through the crowd with a look of intent.

Dara followed suit, her heels forcing her to tread more carefully. 'I'm not sure what I said to bother you, but this is hardly the place to cause a scene.'

Gianni turned his head, still walking. 'You don't need to witness this.'

Leo saw them approach and instantly shooed away the group of people surrounding him. 'Gianni, you're looking a bit more colourful.' He smiled.

The old man jabbed a finger into Leo's chest, standing so close they were almost nose to nose. 'You say you're not playing games, boy? Then explain what kind of agreement you have with this young lady? Do you plan to sell off the only link you have left to your family?'

Leo looked genuinely shocked for a moment. 'Will you keep your voice down?'

Gianni shook his head, a harsh laugh escaping his lips. 'Always worried about your precious image, Leo. I thought you were hurting when you did what you did to Valente Enterprises, but this—' His voice cracked.

'I'm not selling the damned castle,' Leo spat harshly.

'He's not. I'm a wedding planner. We're discussing an event contract.'

'Stay out of this, Dara,' Leo warned.

'And I thought you were just entertaining the lady to charm her into bed,' said Gianni. 'It would be better if you sold it. Rather than make plans to exploit it like a cheap hotel.'

'Nothing is going to be planned in that damned castle—you hear me? It's staying there to rot.'

Dara felt the breath whoosh out of her lungs as she absorbed the reality of that statement. Neither man looked her way as they continued in their stand-off. Thankfully no one had noticed the little drama playing out in this quiet corner of the club.

'Then why is she here?' asked Gianni, voicing Dara's own question.

Leo was silent for a moment, his eyes moving to look at her as if he had just remembered she was there. 'This is none of your business, Gianni.'

Dara watched as the old man's temper faded, to be replaced by a look of genuine hurt. Leo's eyes were so dark they looked almost black in the dim lighting.

Dara spoke up, straightening her shoulders. 'Well, it seems it's none of my business either.'

Refusing to meet Leo's eyes, she looked down.

'Thank you for shedding some light on the situation, Mr Marcello.'

With that, she turned on her heel and strode out of the club.

CHAPTER FOUR

STOPPING TO GRAB her coat and bag from
the cloakroom, Dara willed herself to calm
down. She could feel the tension inside her
stretching to breaking point.

After devoting the entire day working
herself to the bone to impress him…

After spending one hair-raisingly stress-
ful hour on the phone to every major designer, looking for uniforms…

After letting him make her feel self-
conscious…

She honestly thought that if he was to
follow her she might wind up hitting someone for the first time in her life.

She stepped out into the chilly Milan
night, the cool air making her shiver in earnest through the haze of cold anger.

He emerged through the doors behind

her just as explosively as he had the night before. 'Dara, stop walking away and allow me to explain.'

'How long were you planning on stringing me along for?' She spun around to face him.

'Let's not do this on the street.' He looked to where the security guards stood like silent sentries inside the door.

'Oh, excuse me—I forgot all about your precious reputation. Please, do yourself a favour and go back to your adoring public.'

A long dark limo pulled up in front of them, the windows impenetrably black.

'You're not going to get anywhere by standing on the street. My car is right here. I don't want anything else on my conscience tonight.'

'Oh, I think we both know your conscience doesn't exist,' she scoffed.

Still, she frowned. She had forgotten about the trouble getting a taxi in Milan. If he was offering her his limo she would take it without a second thought. Anything to get her away from him as soon as possible.

'Well, it seems you are just as charitable as I thought you'd be, Mr Valente. My humble thanks for this consolation prize.' She opened the door and slid inside to the warm dark interior, her body still shaking with anger.

The door on the opposite side opened suddenly, and her eyes widened as Leo's tall frame slid easily onto the seat next to her.

'What are you doing?' she squeaked.

'I said I'd let you use the limo. I didn't say you would be going alone.' He shrugged one shoulder, banging his knuckles on the driver's window and setting the vehicle into swift motion.

He turned to face her, his voice deeply accented in the limo's quiet, dark interior. 'We are not finished yet, Dara.'

She felt his voice reach across the space between them, warm and seductive. Ignoring the pull, she remained silent and feigned indifference.

'You can ignore me if you like, but I have yet to fulfil my side of our bargain.' He waited for her to speak for a moment before continuing. 'Your work tonight was impressive. You've earned your chance to convince me.'

Indignation won out and she turned to face him. 'Excuse me if I'm suddenly disinclined to pitch to a brick wall.'

'You don't understand the situation with Gianni Marcello.'

He shook his head. That small movement incensed her more than anything else.

'I think I understand perfectly well. The bored playboy decided he'd have some fun while he was in town. An added bonus was the free event consultation. Too bad your friend ruined things before you tried your hand at the final prize, eh?' She crossed her arms defensively around herself.

'What you achieved tonight is unheard of. I wasn't lying when I said you have great talent. You achieved more in seven hours than my team could pull off in three months.'

'That means nothing to me. The only reason I did any of it was to get my contract.'

'My relationship with Gianni is complex. He does not understand some of the choices that I have made. I said what I had to in order to avoid a scene. The truth is I have been considering your proposal.'

Dara watched him silently. This change in tactics was making her head spin.

He sat back in his seat, stretching long muscular legs in front of him with casual ease. 'I'm offering you a chance to convince me. It won't be offered again.'

Dara deliberated for a moment. He had made a fool of her, but he still held the upper hand here. If there was a chance to salvage this wedding contract she had to take it. Much as it irked her to be played with in his little game...much as it wounded her pride.

'The wedding is for a high-profile actress—moderate numbers. Media would be limited to one magazine team. It would be maybe three days from set-up to clean-up, with accommodation required for guests.'

She outlined the finer details of her pitch as clearly and effectively as she could, considering her lack of sleep and the intimate environment. Not to mention the large relaxed male sitting beside her, watching her every movement with interest.

'Sounds like you've thought of everything.' He ran a hand across the stubble on his jaw. 'And it sounds like a mutually beneficial arrangement.'

Dara felt unease prickle at the back of her mind. He had been deathly against any conversation about the castle last night—why the sudden easy consideration of her plans? She *had* done a fantastic job today—that much she could admit. But she wasn't naive enough to overlook the fact that something had to have sparked this sudden change of heart.

'What exactly has changed to make you think twice about rejecting my event?' she asked, watching as he raised his brows a fraction of an inch, narrowing his gaze.

'Maybe I'm hoping to leave you with a better impression of me than the one you have got so far.'

'Somehow I don't think that you care very much about anyone's impression of you.'

He shrugged. 'Depends on the person in

question. But nonetheless you are correct that I have an ulterior motive. I was merely giving you a chance to lay out your proposal beforehand.'

Leo sat forward in his seat, green eyes intently holding her gaze.

'You need my help, Dara. And you have proved just how far you are willing to go in order to get it. I am asking you to go just a little further.'

He laid a hand on the dark leather between them, still holding her gaze. It was a gesture of domination, designed to make her feel trapped, surely? She fought the urge to move back further in her seat.

'How much further are we talking, here?' Dara shook off the mildly indecent thoughts her mind conjured.

Leo seemed to deliberate for a moment, looking out at the passing streets before speaking.

'Do you know much about the newest Lucchesi development?'

Dara thought for a moment, the change in pace addling her already tired mind. 'The island he owns near Lampedone? He's turning it into some sort of self-contained luxury resort, I've heard.'

Leo nodded. 'Despite what you've heard or read, thus far I have made no attempt to expand my empire to Sicily. There is virtually no market for an exclusive brand like mine in any of the larger cities. That was until this Isola project came to light.' He sat forward, gesturing with his hands as he spoke. 'The island will be a hub of exclusive hotels, boutique restaurants. Every inch of real estate will be dedicated to five-star luxury. It's one of a kind.'

'I don't see what your interest in a new real estate development has to do with my wedding contract.' Dara spoke quietly, trying to make sense of his words.

'Umberto Lucchesi is head of the board of directors. He has the final word on all potential investment opportunities. I have made no secret of the fact that I want in on the project, and frankly they need my expertise and influence. That was made clear when the entire board approved my investment. All except Lucchesi.'

She shook her head. 'I'm sorry, but I

don't think my small connection with him would help you to secure a major business deal.'

'All I would need is your presence, Dara. He is notoriously private and only holds meetings in his home or with the board of directors. There is an opera fundraiser at the Teatro Massimo in Palermo tomorrow night. Lucchesi and his wife will be hosting.'

Palermo? Tomorrow night? Dara fought the urge to laugh in disbelief. This was ridiculous. She had flown to Milan for a simple task and now here she was being asked to accompany a notorious playboy to the opera.

'Why exactly would my presence benefit the situation?' she asked rather breathlessly.

'I understand that this is rather unconventional. But I believe meeting with him in a cordial setting, with a familiar face by my side, might make him look upon me more favourably. He sees me as my father's son—a frivolous playboy with no morals. He clearly approves of you if he has worked with you on more than one occasion. Having you on my arm would be greatly beneficial.'

'Are you asking me to pose as your *date*?'

'What other reason would we have for being in Palermo together? It's the most believable scenario.'

Maybe it was tiredness after the past twenty-four hours catching up with her, but Dara felt a wave of hysterical laughter threatening to bubble up to the surface. The thought that anyone would believe a man like Leo Valente was dating a plain Irish nobody like her was absolutely ludicrous.

He continued, oblivious to her stunned reaction. 'You would leave the business talk to me. All I'd need is for you to act as a buffer of sorts. To play on your history with his family. Someone with a personal connection to smooth the way.'

'A buffer? Well that just sounds so flattering...' she muttered.

'You would get all the benefits of being my companion, being a guest at such an exclusive event. It would be an enjoyable evening.'

'Umberto Lucchesi is a powerful man.

He must have good reason not to trust you,' she mused. 'I'm not quite sure I can risk my reputation.'

'I'm a powerful man, Dara. You climbed up a building to get a meeting with me. I'm offering you an opportunity to get exactly what you want. It's up to you if you take it or not.'

The limo came to a stop. Dara looked out at the hotel's dull grey exterior, trying desperately to get a handle on the situation. He was essentially offering her the *castello* on a silver platter. All she had to do was play a part until he got his meeting and she would be done.

'What happens if you're wrong? If having a buffer makes no difference?'

'Let me worry about that. My offer is simple. Come with me to Palermo and I will sign your event contract.'

She thought about the risk of trusting him. He hadn't given her any reason to trust him so far. But what other possible reason could he have for asking her to go with him?

A man like him could have any woman

he wanted, so this wasn't simply about the chemistry between them. She was sure of that.

He must want in on the Lucchesi deal very badly if it had prompted him to consider her event. His initial reaction had been a complete contrast, his blatant refusal so clear. It was a risk to lie to a man like Umberto Lucchesi, but on the scale of things it was more of a white lie. And the alternative meant losing the contract. Losing everything she had worked for.

'If I go with you—' she said it quickly, before she could change her mind '—I want a contract for the *castello* up front.'

Leo felt triumph course through him as he felt Dara's shift towards accepting his offer. He'd seen the uncertainty on her face, knew the difficult position he was placing her in.

'You don't trust me, Dara?'

'Not even a little bit.'

'I would expect nothing less. I will have a contract drawn up by tomorrow. And I promise to return you to your office bright and early on Monday morning.'

'We would be staying in Palermo overnight?'

She asked the question innocently, but he'd seen the telltale movement of her hands in her lap. She was not as unaware of the tension as she made it seem.

'The suite will have more than one bedroom.'

'I want your word that there will be no more of your games. This is a professional arrangement.'

'Are you asking me to behave myself? To ignore the intense attraction between us?' he asked silkily.

'Yes. That's exactly what I'm asking.'

'This is a business arrangement, Dara. You may be posing as my date for the evening, but I can assure you I am capable of separating the two. Whatever impression you might have of me, I can assure you that I am a man of my word when it comes to business.'

Leo rapped the driver's window and the

man got out and held the door of the limousine open for her to exit.

'My plane will leave at noon, so you have plenty of time to get some beauty sleep.'

He watched until she'd disappeared through the doors of the basic hotel. He hadn't lied when he'd said he was capable of separating business from pleasure. He was quite capable of it, usually. But his attraction to her was something that had caught him off guard.

After months of no interest in the opposite sex, this sudden acute awareness was almost painful. And she felt it too—he was quite sure of that. She would prove very useful tomorrow in cornering Lucchesi. But if he was being honest that was not his only objective. He wasn't quite ready to walk away from the challenge she presented just yet.

Maybe it was boredom…maybe his pride was bruised. But something drew him to Dara Devlin more than to any woman he had ever met. She intrigued him and maybe that was why he had insisted on provoking her with those little stunts at the club.

He was a grown man not a teenager, for goodness' sake.

If he wanted to impress her then he had to get on her good side. It was his nature to be rebellious and provocative, but maybe a more subtle approach was needed. Either way, he always got what he wanted. And he was determined to show Dara exactly what she could have if she gave in to temptation.

The car turned sharply onto another narrow backstreet and Dara felt her stomach lurch. She sat bolt upright in the Porsche's deep suede seat, one hand clutching her phone like a talisman, the other holding onto the door for dear life. Leo drove as if he was on the Nürburgring, not the tiny cobbled streets of Palermo.

Rounding the last corner, he pulled the powerful vehicle to a smooth stop. She was out of the car in an instant, straightening her skirt and trying to regain her composure.

'You didn't enjoy the drive?'

Leo handed his keys to the valet and fell into step beside her as she powered up the pathway to the facade of the ancient building they had arrived at.

'I generally prefer to travel at a less ferocious pace.'

She stared up at the historical *palazzo*, amazed that she should be staying in such a place. They walked up marble steps and entered into a bright, ornate lobby. Dara felt her breath catch at the veritable feast of opulent decor.

'I always knew that some of these old palaces had been converted into luxury suites, but I never thought I would see inside one.'

She craned her neck to look up at the ornate ceiling artwork. Most of the original features had been preserved, and it was like stepping through a doorway into the eighteenth century.

The interior of the apartment was just as flamboyant as the lobby. Decorated in traditional Baroque fashion, it had high ceilings and large ornate chandeliers, with a sizeable balcony overlooking the terracotta rooftops of the city.

Leo guided her through the living area to

a set of floor-to-ceiling double doors. 'Your room is through here. Your bag should have been brought up by now.'

'Already?' She raised her brows with surprise as he opened the double doors and, sure enough, her small black case was at the foot of the bed.

'I expect efficiency wherever I go.' He shrugged.

Dara took in the gigantic four-poster bed, draped with deep red velvet hangings and a gold-embroidered coverlet. It was the kind of bed that demanded lovemaking and romance. Too bad it would be getting neither tonight.

It suddenly dawned on her that in a few hours she would be posing as Leo Valente's date. And sleeping under the same roof as him. The insane urge to run screaming from the building was tempting, but she stood her ground. *Remember the goal here, Devlin.* One white lie and the *castello* was hers.

'We leave for the opera house at seven. Will you find something to wear in time?'

'I once sourced seven bridesmaids'

dresses the day before a wedding I was planning. In mint green, might I add,' she professed proudly.

He didn't respond with his usual snark, instead taking a quick look at the screen of his phone. 'I have some business to attend to, but feel free to indulge yourself. Shoes, jewellery. Whatever you desire.'

He took a sleek silver card from his wallet and held it out to her.

'I can pay for my own clothes, but I appreciate the gesture.' She pushed the card back towards him.

Leo scowled at her. 'Fine. I will have the car collect us at seven.'

He left, closing the doors of the bedroom behind him.

Dara wondered at the change in his playful demeanour. Perhaps he was edgy about the significance of tonight.

She would need to get a start on shopping, but first things first… She kicked off her shoes and threw herself back onto the bed with a contented sigh of appreciation. It was like sinking into a cloud. She briefly imagined what it might be like not to be alone in this bed. To have a warm body next to her, touching her in all the right places.

What on earth was happening to her? She was going to have to keep her guard up around him. Her usually controlled libido seemed to be coming out of its enforced hibernation.

He wasn't even her usual type.

She thought of her ex-fiancé and his neat brown hair, his perfectly ironed shirts and slacks. Dan would never have looked at her the way Leo did. As though she was the most attractive woman in the room. Even before he'd found out she was as barren as the desert.

The ugly phrase jarred her momentarily. It was the phrase she had heard Daniel use to her father in a conversation she had never been meant to hear.

Thoughts of her past pressed through her control, filling her chest with emotion. The news that she would never have children had shaken her to her core. She had always prided herself on not being needy in her relationships, unlike most of her girlfriends. Dan was the only man she had ever slept with. Their sex life had been nothing spectacular, but she'd told herself that their mental connection was worth much more than the lack of wow factor in the bedroom. Apparently he hadn't felt the same.

Dara shook off the irritation that always followed thoughts about their break-up. Moving to stand in front of the floor-length mirror by the bed, she frowned at her reflection. She wasn't sexy—she knew that. But once upon a time she had felt moderately attractive…she had accepted male attention graciously.

She was by no means vain. She knew that she had a slim figure and long legs, but her features were plain and her chest far too small. Why a man like Leo would ever be attracted to her, she didn't know. Perhaps it was the simple fact that she had made it clear that nothing would happen between them.

But the problem was the longer they were together, the more she *wanted* something to happen.

She walked away from the mirror, trying her best not to groan. What was it about this man that made her second guess herself? Leo Valente was trouble with a capital T, and she needed to keep her own attraction under control if she had any hope of keeping his at bay.

Leo grabbed two flutes of champagne from a passing waiter and returned to his seat in the private box.

He'd seen that Dara had taken out her phone and was busily tapping away.

'The tech-junkie look isn't exactly what I want in a date,' he scolded.

'Just give me a minute and I'll be done.' She tapped a few more times on the screen.

'You're on my time tonight, Dara.' He took the phone swiftly from her grasp, putting it in his inner pocket. 'You can have it back after the opera if you behave.'

She stared at him. 'That is a very high-handed approach to regaining my attention.'

'You don't find it charming?' He placed a flute of champagne in her hand.

'Not even a little bit.' She straightened, sipping her champagne and looking pointedly away from him down towards the crowds swarming below them in the theatre.

Leo felt more than a little irked at her dismissal. He had spent all afternoon on conference calls so he could free up some time. Only to be coolly ignored by her from the moment he'd collected her from the *palazzo*.

She looked spectacular, with her blonde hair swept back from her face in a neat chignon, revealing delicate diamond-drop earrings. Her gown was elegant and refined—a swathe of pale silver that formed a seductive heart shape at the front, showing just enough skin to leave a little mystery.

He moved closer to her, speaking quietly. 'I would imagine you prefer a very docile man. One you can organise and control, perhaps?'

'I don't really have a preference.' She shrugged one delicate shoulder. 'I have a very busy career that fulfils me. Dating is not high on my agenda.'

'Again with the agenda, Dara? You seem to have it all figured out into neat little boxes. It sounds so perfectly perfect.'

'You're mocking me, but there is a lot to be said for having a plan.'

'When building a nightclub empire, definitely. But everything else is free fall to me. I enjoy surprises. If it weren't for surprises we wouldn't be here tonight.'

'Back to the point: when will I be expected to sidetrack the Lucchesi's?'

'Not until the first interlude. Follow my lead and don't go off script.'

Dara fought the urge to make a snappy retort, instead relaxing as the music started up. The ancient opera house was beautiful, with its iconic gold architecture and deep red velvet curtains. She had promised herself years ago that she would see a show at the Teatro Massimo—it was on her list of tourist-type things to do while she was living here. A list that she never seemed to get to with her workload…

As the curtain came down for the first interlude she felt butterflies in her stomach. Leo gestured for her to follow him out into the crowd mingling outside the doorway. This was it. The moment of truth. He laid one hand at the small of her back as they walked down the corridors towards the royal box, where the Lucchesi family was seated. The heat from his palm seared into her skin, making those butterflies flap even faster.

A group of people were gathered around the entrance, talking loudly about the performance. One woman stood out, her opulent diamond jewellery outshone only by what had to be the most eye-blurringly white fur stole that Dara had ever seen.

Leo caught Dara's eye, gesturing for her to step forward and intercept the woman's attention.

Dara pasted on her most brilliant smile as Gloria Lucchesi came out of the crowd, embracing her warmly. She tried not to look at Leo, noting the smug expression on his face.

'Dara, darling—what are you doing out in public without your headset?' The older woman joked.

Dara laughed obligingly at the jibe, feeling unease as Leo stepped right up to her side, sliding his hand around her waist possessively.

'I'm here with my…my date, Leo Valente.'

Her voice stumbled over the words, her heart hammering in her chest. Whether it was the effect of lying so brazenly, or the result of being touched so intimately, Dara felt as if her heart was about to leap out of her chest.

Her skittishness evaporated once she noticed that Gloria Lucchesi had quite literally frozen in place, her hand clutching at her necklace in a gesture that was much more than simple surprise. Dara felt a sense of foreboding as Umberto Lucchesi came to stand beside his wife, his features ruddy with barely leashed anger.

Gloria placed a hand on her husband's arm before speaking to Dara directly. 'Miss Devlin, can you please explain what you are doing here with my husband's nephew?'

Umberto Lucchesi looked like a man ready to pounce.

Leo continued to stare, unblinking. 'How nice to see you, Uncle.'

'How dare you ambush me at a charity function?' the older man practically hissed under his breath, looking around the hall to see they were not being overheard.

'I bought a ticket—just like everyone else here.'

True to form, Aunt Gloria stepped forward to calm the situation. 'Umberto, please stop being so dramatic,' she chastised. Her tone was one of calm confidence. 'My husband forgets that he is in the middle of the Teatro Massimo, not shouting in a boardroom.'

Gloria placed a friendly hand on Dara's arm. Leo noted Dara's polite smile, her gentle tone as she defused the situation with questions about Gloria's daughters.

Umberto remained silent and continued to stare at him across the narrow hallway.

'We will not do this here, Valente,' he hissed.

'Most certainly not,' Gloria interjected. 'It's high time you ridiculous men quit this feud and showed each other a little forgiveness. Leonardo, I want to welcome you home to Sicily, darling. I have missed you.'

'Thank you, Zia, I'm afraid your husband doesn't quite feel the same.'

'That's an understatement,' Umberto scoffed.

Gloria spoke directly to him. 'Come to our villa tomorrow evening for dinner. You can talk business then. For now, let us all enjoy the rest of the evening.' She guided her husband into the throng of people, looking back to wink at Dara.

Leo smiled at Dara. That had gone just the way he'd planned it. A private meeting attained, on Lucchesi's home turf. But Dara frowned, turning back towards the box. Leo followed, confused at her sudden change in mood.

Dara waited until they were back in the box before turning to him. She pressed one accusatory finger into his shoulder. The gesture made his eyes widen.

'You could have warned me that I was walking into an episode of a *soap opera*, for goodness' sake.'

'I didn't think it would benefit the situation if you were aware of my history with Umberto.'

'No, you didn't think it would benefit *you*.' She turned away, fuming. 'How did I not know that you were related? How is it not common knowledge?'

'He is my mother's younger brother. He made a point of removing himself from any connection to the Valente name when my mother passed away.' He spoke matter-of-factly, anger evident in the hard set of his jaw.

Dara felt her anger deflate, taken by surprise by his candid statement. 'That must have been very difficult.'

'My mother died quite suddenly—she was only thirty-eight. The funeral was an ugly affair, and her family blamed my father. And me.'

'Goodness, she was very young. Life can be cruel sometimes.'

Leo waved off her gentle comments. 'I am merely divulging the facts to you—not looking for sympathy. I've had twelve years to get over it.'

He shoved his hands into the pockets of

his designer tuxedo, a sardonic tilt to his brow. This was a man who kept his true feelings buried. She couldn't imagine revealing her own painful memories in such a matter-of-fact fashion.

Dara thought of the way the two men had just stood toe to toe, eyes spitting fire at one another, in the glamorous gilded hallway of the *teatro*.

'Leo, I've helped you to get your meeting. I've fulfilled my part of our bargain. We agreed that I would act as your date for tonight only.'

'I can't go alone to dinner. You will accompany me to keep up the pretence that we are an item. Gloria likes you, and she is the key to keeping the peace.'

Dara shifted uneasily on her feet, smoothing a hand over the smooth pearl satin of her gown. She had felt like a princess earlier, walking down the steps of the *palazzo* to find Leo leaning against the door of the limo, dressed in a perfectly tailored black tuxedo. He looked sinfully handsome and powerful, and it was doing all kinds of strange things to her breathing every time he held her arm or looked at her with that smouldering dark gaze.

She needed to cut her losses before she did something stupid. One more night with Leo was a risk she couldn't take.

He was watching her intently. 'What is it that worries you, *carina*? That they won't believe we are a couple? Because that won't be a problem.'

'It's too risky. We know nothing about each other. What if they ask questions?' she argued.

'They won't need to.' He stepped closer. 'Dara, we practically crackle every time we are alone together. The chemistry between us is quite obvious.'

'It is?' Dara felt a little dazed under his scrutiny.

'Oh, yes.' He lowered his voice. 'We naturally react to each other. That's not something that can be feigned easily and we can use it to our advantage.'

'I don't see how arguing with each other will make it seem that we are a couple.'

She turned away, fighting against herself. She was enjoying this little charade they had embarked upon. It was beginning to feel like an alternative reality to her hectic and rather solitary life in Syracuse.

'Tension can be interpreted in many ways.'

Leo stepped behind her, close enough that she could feel his breath below her ear.

'Physical signs are the first things that people notice. Unconscious displays of intimacy.' He reached for her hand, lacing his fingers through hers.

Dara's breath caught in her chest at the effect of the innocent yet explosive contact on her already heightened senses.

'So we hold hands and everything will be okay?'

'There is no need to go over the top when subtlety will work much better. I might rest a hand on the small of your back while we talk. Display possession.'

Dara tried to focus on his words, but all she could think about was how hard and warm his hand felt surrounding hers. It had been so long since she'd had her hand held.

She shook off that warm fuzzy thought. She tried to seem blasé, barely noticing his movement until she felt his hand slide sensually low on her spine.

'What are you doing?' she squeaked.

'Dara, no one will believe this if your voice rises an entire octave every time I touch you,' he whispered in her ear as they were rejoined by the other guests in their box.

She took the opportunity to retake her seat and study the programme while she calmed her erratic breathing. The music started and Leo sat beside her. Very close beside her.

'Let's try this again,' he whispered softly.

His hand came to rest upon hers in her lap, his fingers massaging the back of her palm idly, just as a lover's might. He looked straight ahead, focusing on the beautiful performance, completely unaffected by their contact.

She was suddenly very aware of her breathing as she tried to concentrate on the stage below.

His fingers laced through hers as his

head tilted and he whispered in her ear. 'Much better, Dara, a perfect balance between quiet disdain and shivering anticipation.'

'I did not shiver,' she hissed, turning to find his eyes filled with mirth.

The couple next to them tutted with disapproval.

'You're being deliberately disruptive.' She shook her head, focusing on the show below.

'I can't help it.' He tilted his head again, his attention now completely focused on her.

'Well, try harder,' she scolded, folding her hands in her lap tightly. 'This isn't the place to teach me how to lie effectively. I haven't even agreed to continue this little charade.'

'You're right.' He stood up, grabbing her by the hand and speaking quietly to the couple behind them. 'Excuse us—my beautiful companion isn't quite feeling herself.' He pulled her up from her seat easily and motioned for her to precede him out through the door of the box.

Dara exited into the corridor, turning to face him as he closed the door behind him. 'I didn't mean that we had to leave,' she said, exasperated.

'My attention wasn't exactly on the show.' He stepped closer. 'Something occurred to me in there.'

Dara watched as he took another step, bringing him so close they were almost chest to chest. His eyes didn't leave hers as he leaned closer, his gaze sweeping over her lips with clear intent. The thought occurred to her that she was going to let him kiss her. Even worse—she wanted him to.

'What occurred to you?' she whispered, her tongue sneaking out to dampen her lips before she could stop herself.

He followed the movement eagerly. 'You have no reason to help me after tonight.'

'I suppose you're right.' She shook off the feeling of disappointment at his words. He was correct. After tonight they had no reason to continue to work together except for maybe exchanging emails about the *castello*.

'What if I offered you more than a contract for your celebrity wedding?' he asked quietly.

Dara felt her pulse quicken at the word *more*.

'I've been thinking… The castle is virtually abandoned, with no purpose. Your vision for this wedding will bring vitality to it again. It might even help bring some revenue to Monterocca. God knows they need it, being so far from the busier tourist resorts.'

'I'm flattered you paid so much attention to my slideshow.' She smiled.

'I can offer you exclusive rights to hold a small amount of select weddings at the *castello*. I will hire you to oversee the renovations and ensure it is fit for purpose again.'

'Leo, that would be…amazing…' she breathed.

'I want nothing more to do with the place once this deal is finalised. So it's not a selfless act. I trust that you will do a good job, Dara?'

'I assure you that you will have nothing

to worry about,' she gushed, the excitement of his revelation taking her completely by surprise.

'You will accompany me tomorrow evening, then?' he said plainly.

Dara laughed. 'I suppose I'll have to now.'

'It will be the last thing I ask of you.'

His expression was earnest as they made their way down the corridor to the grand hallway and out towards the waiting car.

The thought of spending another evening as the focus of his attention, of having him touch her and speak to her like a lover, made her feel uneasy.

She stayed silent on the drive back to the apartment, her thoughts still frazzled from their encounter in the opera box. He had barely touched her and she'd been on the verge of throwing herself at him. She had been so sure he was about to kiss her in the corridor.

The fear of being branded a liar by Umberto Lucchesi was nothing compared to the fear of being kissed by Leo Valente. He hadn't kissed her yet, but with an entire evening planned in his company tomorrow, surely it was inevitable that he would.

It had been so long since she had kissed anyone she was afraid she'd forgotten how to do it. Maybe it was best to treat it as a task. She never went into tasks unprepared. She would treat it like pulling off a sticking plaster. Quick and painless. After all, the fear of the unknown was usually worse than the act itself.

When they entered the apartment Leo pulled off his bow tie in one movement, throwing it on a side table and moving towards the door of his bedroom.

'Wait.' She spoke as confidently as she could muster. 'I just want to try something first.'

On steady feet she walked to him, seeing his eyes widen as she stepped close. Her lips touched his—hesitantly at first, then fully. He smelled amazing this close, and his lips were hard and hot under hers. She stepped back before she could get too comfortable, feeling her legs tremble just a little bit as she put some distance between them once more.

'There—that's the awkward first kiss over and done with.' She smiled, proud of herself for finding a logical way to deal with an uncomfortable situation.

Leo stayed silent for a moment, his expression entirely unreadable. Then he took a step, closing the space between them. 'If you wanted to try it out, all you had to do was ask, Dara.'

'It was just a practice run. For tomorrow.' She felt her body react as he closed in once more. As if her skin remembered him, was begging him to step closer again. What on earth had come over her?

'In that case I think we need another try.'

His lips were on hers before she could formulate a reply. But this kiss was not simple and exploratory, as hers had been. His mouth was hard on hers, his lips pressing with an urgency she had never felt before. She felt it too. It was as though the entire world had fallen away and all that mattered was this. Feeling his mouth on hers, his hands wrapping around her waist.

His wicked tongue traced a trail of fire

across her lips, demanding access. She tried to think straight. This was all wrong. It had started as a simple kiss and now suddenly she was being ravished.

She tilted her head back and he took advantage. His hands moved from her waist down to her bottom, holding her to him. She had never felt awareness like this before. The feel of his hard chest against her own made her nipples peak with need. Her breasts felt heavy, aching with the demand to be in the open air. She felt wanton and free and prayed her sanity wouldn't return any time soon. She let her own tongue move against his, following the rhythm and feeling the hard weight of his arousal press against her.

He began kissing a passionate trail of fire down the soft skin of her neck. Dara moaned at the sensation, shocked at the sensation of molten heat building between her thighs.

She wanted him more than she had ever wanted any man before. His smell, his touch was driving her so wild she could barely think. All she could hear was the sound of her heart beating loud in her ears. His breath was equally as ragged as he nibbled her earlobe and pulled the neckline of her dress down so that it rested high on her waist.

Dara felt her body react reflexively, softening to him, unconsciously offering more. Cohesive thought left her as she gave in to the warmth of his hard muscular body surrounding her. He pushed against her shoulders until she was lying on the plush sofa in the living room. His mouth lowered to the sensitive skin of her breasts and the last remnant of her resolve seemed to melt away. All she could feel was him and the wild, primal movements of his lips and teeth as they tasted and teased her.

His tongue circled one tip as his thumb and forefinger slowly tortured the other. She writhed under his touch, her hips arching up to meet the hard ridge below his abdomen.

He raised his head to kiss her once more, his lips softer this time as he continued to tease one nipple with his fingers. His hand moved lower, tracing a path down her stomach to her lower thigh. He pulled the silken material of her dress up so that it bunched around her hips. His fingers were stroking up the skin of her thigh as his lips continued to demand brutal response from her own. She grabbed a fistful of thick dark hair, feeling a wave of triumph as he growled and kissed her harder.

His hand caressed her, higher still, cupping her over the thin lace of her underwear. She felt her stomach clench in response and raised her hips to meet him, feeling his fingers press against that sensitive part of her through the gauzy material. She needed his skin on hers—needed the release that she could feel building.

He growled low in his throat as she put her hand over his, guiding him towards the edge of the French lace, begging him to reach inside. His hands were everywhere…his lips were in her ear murmuring something incomprehensible in Italian.

He stilled momentarily, his hips pressed hard against her as she lay spread underneath him on the sofa. '*Dio*, you make me forget myself,' he breathed harshly. 'We have to slow down for a moment... I need to get some protection from the bedroom.' He traced a trail down her neck, licking the hollow of her throat.

Dara felt as though a bucket of ice had been thrown over her as she realised just what had been about to happen. She barely knew him and she had been about to have wild, unprotected sex with him on a sofa. Where was her self-control now?

Clambering out from underneath his powerful frame, she fought against the emotion building in her chest.

'What's wrong?'

He held on to her, his powerful bare chest still burning against her skin. She pushed more forcefully this time, noting his expression turn quickly to confusion as he moved, letting her struggle to her feet.

'I can't do this,' she breathed, tugging at her wrinkled dress to cover her exposed flesh. She felt completely bared, mortified at her own behaviour.

Leo stood up, then remained deathly still, his breathing laboured and heat high on his cheekbones. 'You're the one who walked over to *me*, Dara.'

'I didn't kiss you like—like that,' she stammered, trying desperately to get her ragged breathing under control.

'Are you angry because I kissed you or because you liked it a little too much?'

'We barely know each other. I don't do things like this.'

It wasn't a lie. The thought of casual sex was an entirely foreign concept to her. But right now her panic had nothing to do with morals and more to do with the thought of getting close to any man again.

'I make you lose control, Dara. That's what you don't like. I don't know why you're so afraid of letting yourself have pleasure.'

'Don't assume that you know me—or how I feel.' She shook her head.

He didn't know what it was like to have your life plan taken away without warning. To have a man you trusted shatter your entire self-worth to pieces. She could very easily use sex with Leo to unwind and forget about the memories bubbling to the surface. But she wouldn't, and that was her choice to deal with.

Leo shrugged with finality, clearly done with arguing over the matter. 'Fair enough. Let me know when you change your mind.'

She walked to her bedroom door, looking back one more time to where he stood like a Greek god in the middle of the ornate living room.

'I won't.'

'It's so nice to have our Leo back—isn't it, girls?'

The Lucchesi family sat together in the formal sitting room of their historic Palermo villa. Umberto Lucchesi was known for collecting what he perceived to be pieces amongst his country's greatest treasures. His love of historic architecture was inherited from his aristocratic lineage.

Gloria smiled indulgently as her two teenaged daughters nodded politely in unison, and Leo laid his hand on top of Dara's, feeling her tense slightly. Her face belied her discomfort but she smiled at him—a warm smile no doubt intended to display affection.

He could see the confusion in her eyes, sense how distant she had become since last night. His night had consisted of a very cold shower and a much needed glass of whisky.

She had enjoyed kissing him, and what had followed afterwards, much more than she'd intended to. He remembered the way the soft curves of her breasts had felt beneath his palms. She was a well of heat under all that ice. But now, knowing how good her skin tasted, it made it even more difficult to sit close to her without throwing her over his shoulder like a caveman and finding the nearest bed.

The only problem now was that he wondered if he would ever get enough. She was intoxicating. Since they had arrived at dinner he'd found himself touching her at every excuse. He had no doubt that she would come to him before the night was through—he could see it in the sultry way she kept regarding him every time she thought he wasn't looking. She was at war with her precious rules, but he had a feeling he knew who would win out.

She shot him another glance as he laid his hand against the warmth of her back.

His uncle interrupted his erotic thoughts. 'Leo, let's take a cigar outside and let the women chat.' Umberto gestured for him to follow him out onto the back terrace.

Leo regretfully closed the door behind them, leaving Dara inside to talk with his aunt and cousins. It was clear that his uncle knew why he was here. He had gotten him alone…now all he needed to do was appeal to the man's logic and speed up this deal. Then he could focus on Dara.

'So, nephew. You've played your hand well.' Umberto lit a cigar, letting the smoke billow in the air between them. He offered one to Leo.

Leo refused with a wave of his hand.

Umberto huffed out a cloud of smoke, looking up at the darkening evening sky. 'So, tell me, is using the blonde a vital part of your plan or just a little extra fun while you're here?'

'Dara and I have been seeing each other for a while now.'

'Spare me the lies, Valente. You know I don't take well to them.' The older man scowled. 'She's too good for a low life like you. She's got character.'

Leo felt a prickle of unease at the back of his neck. 'Umberto, whatever happened between my father and you is history. I am the furthest thing from him there is.'

'I can tell by your reputation that you have no value for family. That was Valente's worst trait. A Sicilian man puts his family first.'

'My choice of lifestyle is irrelevant. I am the most obvious choice for your development. It's clear to everyone around you and yet you refuse to cut me in. I have the expertise and the resources.'

'I'm not talking about the womanising. Although I do prefer to do business with family men who know the true meaning of responsibility.' Umberto narrowed his eyes, glowering at Leo with a look of unbridled anger. 'You want to know why I'm blocking this deal? I refuse to do business with someone who treats their own flesh and blood like dirt.'

Leo felt the comment cut him deep. He knew Umberto was alluding to his mother. To the way she had been treated by his father—and by Leo, to a certain extent.

'Your father sent my sister into an early grave. The Valente name means nothing to me but selfishness and betrayal.'

'My mother put herself into that grave, Uncle. She committed suicide. She was not the woman you think she was.'

'She was not perfect, no. But she deserved better than to be locked away like a dirty little secret.'

Leo felt the pain of his uncle's words cut to his core. His mother *had* deserved better—they both had. The only person to blame for the life they'd led was his father. But he refused to argue over a bunch of ghosts when his goal was within touching distance. Memories belonged in the past, where they couldn't hurt anybody.

'I'm not here to talk about ancient history. I'm here to talk about the Isola project. I thought that by coming here peacefully, healing the rift between us, we could finally see each other as equals.'

'We will never be equals as long as a Valente owns Lucchesi land.'

Leo thought of the *castello* in Monterocca. His mother's family had owned Castello Bellamo for hundreds of years until she'd married a Valente and signed it away.

He spoke quietly, aware of Umberto's unbridled anger at what he perceived to be yet another slight on his family name. 'I am half-Lucchesi, remember?'

Umberto shook his head.

'My mother would not be happy to know her brother was treating her son this way, Zio.'

Umberto raised one silvery brow. 'Don't play on my sentimentality. It doesn't exist.'

Leo was exasperated. The man was just throwing block after block at him, leaving no room to negotiate. 'What must I do to prove myself?'

'You know what I want. The same thing

I told your father I wanted the day he put my sister in the ground.'

Leo ran a hand down his face. He'd had a feeling it might come to this. 'The *castello* is my birthright.'

'It was built with Lucchesi blood. My family have far more right to Bellamo.'

'You're asking me to part with the place I called home for most of my childhood.'

'If it holds such sentimental value for you why have you left it to rot? You want in on the Isola project? You know what *I* want.'

The older man walked back inside, leaving Leo alone on the terrace with nothing but the sound of the waves rushing against the rocks in the gulf.

Too much quiet made him irritable, and he was grateful when Dara came to find him moments later.

'How did it go?' she enquired.

'As well as I imagined it would.' He shrugged. 'He has made it clear what it will take to let me in on the deal.'

'Is it something you can do?' she asked innocently, handing him a glass of wine.

'It would complicate a lot of things. Upset some people.'

He thought of Dara's face when he told her of his plan for the *castello*. He had heard her on the phone to her client, confirming their contract details. He had offered Dara a complete solution to her problems—a chance to further her business to the next level and avoid ruin. How was he going to tell her that he had to take it all away?

Their contract had loopholes in his favour—he had made sure of that in case it came to this. He had known there was a possibility that Umberto was using the Isola deal to leverage him into signing over the castle, but he hadn't planned on caring about who it might affect.

Dara looked at him thoughtfully. 'You want that deal badly enough to have accepted my event pitch. I don't see what can be so important that you would consider walking away from it now?'

Leo knew she had no idea what she was talking about, but she was right. They didn't know each other well enough for him to take her feelings into account. He had no reason to feel guilty. The loss of the venue might cause her trouble, but he would pay her off. Make sure he lessened the financial blow.

He wouldn't tell her straight away. He would wait at least until he had made his decision.

Dara noticed the stern set of Leo's jaw as they got into the limo. It had been a long evening of polite conversation. The kind of conversation that arose when there was a lot of tension in the air. She noticed that the air of mischief that normally surrounded him had evaporated, to be replaced with a brooding distance.

She found herself wondering at his change in mood, willing him to say something inappropriate and break the silence. She had spent the entire night arguing all the reasons why she shouldn't just cross the hall and slip into his bed. It had been sheer torture, with every fibre in her body urging her to give in to the way he made her feel.

'You keep looking at me,' he said darkly. 'Something to say?'

Dara raised her brows at his tone. 'I was just wondering why you were sitting there like a petulant child all of a sudden.'

'I'm not in the mood for this right now,' he warned.

'It's okay for you to be a jerk, but when it's given back you get annoyed?' She laughed, trying to lighten the mood.

'I was told not to be playful, if I remember correctly. Once the show was over. Or do you forget last night already?'

Dara felt heat creep into her cheeks. How could she ever forget last night? The memory of his mouth devouring hers, his hand sliding between her thighs, had kept her awake most of the night. She had been unable to sleep, knowing he was so near, confused at the sudden longing consuming her. It was *not* how she usually reacted to men—not since she had made the decision never to be with a man again.

She was unable to think around him and unable to resist the temptation he offered.

'Like I said, I'm in no mood to play

games.' He stared out of the window, oblivious to the nature of her thoughts.

'What if I'm not playing games any more?' She spoke quietly, not quite knowing what she'd been about to say until it had already left her lips. 'What if I've changed my mind, Leo?'

Leo watched her for a moment, moving his hand to rest it casually on her thigh. 'I think that maybe you need to spell it out for me, *carina*. In case I am getting the wrong idea.'

With shaky fingers she rested her hand on top of his. Anchoring him there. This was madness. She was supposed to move away, to make a snarky comment or give him the cold shoulder. Not hold his hand like a wanton.

That was the problem, though. She *felt* wanton.

She felt more sexually charged than she had ever felt in her entire relationship with her ex-fiancé. With Dan it had been mutual respect, puppy love.

This was raw lust.

He was completely still, watching in-

tently for her reaction. She could feel his
gaze burning through her. She stopped
thinking, grabbed the front of his shirt and
pressed her lips hard to his.

terrify her reaction. She could feel his gaze burning through her. She stopped mid-climb, gripped the front of his shirt and pressed her free hand to his...

CHAPTER FIVE

LEO FELT THE LAST remnant of his restraint disappear in a haze of heat, as he ran his hands up her sides, his mouth devouring hers. All the pent-up frustration came pouring out of them both as her hands found his hair and she ran her fingers through it, anchoring his head close as he leaned down to kiss her neck.

He began to undo the top few buttons on her blouse and felt her hesitate.

He raised a brow in silent question.

She answered by pulling his head back up and kissing him again. He growled low in his throat, lifting her off the seat and onto his lap. He moulded her curves to him, bunching her skirt up high on her hips and running his palms down the length of her thighs.

'God, you are perfect.'

He groaned, cupping both breasts in his hands and kneading gently. He tilted his hips upwards, moulding their bodies together in a way that made her gasp. He could feel the moisture between her thighs already. She was hot and burning for him.

'We shouldn't be doing this back here,' she breathed. 'The driver might see.'

He ignored her whisper and moved against her again, smiling when she groaned even louder.

'I think you're enjoying the risk.'

'Yes…' she murmured, her eyes closing in a sensual haze as he moved against her in a steady rhythm.

Leo felt victorious as he watched her lose control and give in to the pleasure he was giving her. He pulled her bra down part way, exposing her nipples to him.

'Beautiful…' he murmured, taking one hardened peak into his mouth, then the other.

The limo drove onto rougher terrain and their bodies moved together with the vibrations as he feasted on her as if she was a dessert. His erection moved against her core, torturing them both with the delicious friction.

He vaguely heard Dara curse, felt her body grow tense as he bit down gently on her nipple. Her sudden shuddering release took them both completely by surprise, making her collapse on top of him in a daze of ragged breathing.

'*Dio*, that was the most erotic thing I have ever seen,' he murmured, kissing a trail down her neck.

Dara sat astride him, with her hands still clasped behind his neck. He shifted under her, painfully aware of his rock-hard erection still pressing insistently against her moistened underwear.

She shifted back on his lap, her cheeks rosy from the effects of her orgasm. Her shy smile was breathtaking as she reached down, placing her hand on the hard ridge of his jeans and biting her lower lip as he groaned in response.

Seeing, once again, how much he affected her was more than he could handle. It was like a drug. Now that he had tried it, he just wanted more. The thought of taking her here on the back seat of the limo, in the darkness, almost made him come on the spot.

With extreme restraint Leo placed his hand on top of Dara's, just as she began to lower the zip of his jeans.

She froze, confused as to why they were stopping.

'We are just about to arrive back at the *palazzo*,' he said, smiling at her evident disappointment.

He had succeeded in his efforts to seduce her. She was now his for the taking. And yet he felt the unfamiliar tug of his conscience, threatening to rain down on his lust.

Dara slid off his lap and began closing the buttons of her white blouse with shaky fingers. Her hair was in a tangle around her shoulders…her skirt had twisted around her waist. He had ravished her in the back seat of a moving vehicle and now, in true Valente fashion, he was planning on taking what he wanted before casting her aside.

She would want nothing more to do with

him if he took his uncle's deal. Umberto's words repeated in his mind: he was just like his father. The thought gave the same effect as if he had just doused himself with ice water.

She smiled seductively at him as they walked side by side up the marble steps of the *palazzo*.

Leo hesitated just inside the doorway. 'I think…that you should make your own way up from here.' He avoided her eyes.

'You're not coming upstairs?' she asked, confused at his sudden coldness. She'd clearly presumed they would continue their encounter, after what had just occurred in the limo.

She didn't realise that it was taking every fibre of his self-control not to carry her up to that ridiculously erotic bed of hers and make love to her all night long. Her lips were rosy from his kisses, her hair deliciously mussed. And once again that lacy bra was taunting him through her crisp white shirt.

'I have some things to get done before we head down to Ragusa tomorrow.'

He avoided her gaze, motioning to the valet, who handed him the keys to his Porsche. A drive might clear his head of this ridiculous guilt. And rid him of the ghosts that taunted his every thought.

'Will you be gone long?' she asked.

Leo continued to walk away, refusing to turn around in case he changed his mind. 'I'll see you at breakfast tomorrow, Dara. Sleep well.'

Their drive to the province of Ragusa was made mostly in silence, except for a brief stop for lunch at a roadside café. In less than three hours they reached the shores of the Ionian sea, and a further twenty minutes saw them make their way up the long stretch of coastal road and enter the small sleepy town of Monterocca.

They continued around the winding road to where the cliffs began to lower to sandy beaches and small fishing docks. As they turned the final bend around the headland Dara took a deep intake of breath. It was spectacular.

The castle stood high on a rocky promontory, dominating the surrounding landscape with its high turrets and imposing boundary walls. As they drove through the stone pillared entry Dara felt suddenly dwarfed by the enormity of the place.

She had only seen pictures before now, and photographs were nothing when confronted with the real thing. The stone walls seemed to glow pink in some places, with medieval turrets providing the highest points. The long straight avenue from the main road was rough and untamed. Wild foliage seemed to sweep in and engulf the car entirely at some points. Finally they reached a wide cobbled courtyard with a circular fountain set in the middle. Crumbling statues stood haphazardly all around, some missing their heads, some missing entire limbs.

Dara stepped out of the car and craned her neck to look up at the majestic stonework that decorated the entrance. This close, she could see the complete disrepair the castle had been left in. Chunks of stone had fallen down from the walls in some places. The windows seemed black with dust, and grime and weeds grew from every crevice. All the same, it was a powerful feeling to be surrounded by so much history.

'This place is *breathtaking*.' She sighed, busy taking in every tiny detail of the facade. She pointed to a wing that stretched out at an unusual angle from the main square tower. 'This part isn't medieval, is it?' she asked curiously. Her knowledge of architecture was pretty basic—she generally left historical details to the experts.

He rounded the car to stand next to her, crossing his arms over his chest and leaning casually against the door. 'The whole place is just one big patchwork of various eras. I never thought it was particularly beautiful.'

She shook her head with disbelief. 'How can you say that? It's the imperfections that make it so eye-catching.'

He was wearing sunglasses, but she could still see the sardonic tilt of his brow as he turned to face her. 'So your Hollywood actress is booking it based on all its eye-catching imperfections, is that right?'

'Actually, I think she wants it because her first film was about a Sicilian prince. They filmed in Palermo, but that particular castle was demolished. This one is apparently quite similar.' She shrugged. 'Either way, I don't argue with good publicity.'

He made a grunting sound of accord and took a set of keys from his pocket. He didn't speak another word, still in the same distracted mood as the night before.

They made their way inside the main entryway to a great hall with a ceiling that had to be at least three storeys high. The windows were so filthy, barely any light could get in.

Leo had told her that the housekeeping team consisted of a local woman, Maria, and her husband, who took care of basic tasks. From what she could tell they had just done their best to stop the grounds from being overrun with weeds and keep the dust as minimal as possible with the castle closed up for so long.

'Right, let's get this over with,' Leo said roughly.

Dara took out the clipboard she had

brought with her to take notes, shrugging when he looked at her curiously. 'I thought I might as well jot down my ideas as we go.'

'Always so efficient.' He sighed. 'Don't fall behind. Believe me, you *will* get lost.'

Their voices echoed loudly off the high stone walls as he showed her around the lower level of the main wing. The place was huge, and already she knew she really would be lost in a moment if she didn't follow closely behind him.

She ran her finger along a dusty sideboard, looking upon a row of small framed photographs of a young Leo. He was curly-haired, with emerald-green eyes, smiling mischievously into the camera.

Dara couldn't help but smile down at the photos. 'I cannot believe you lived in a place like this as a child. It must have been one big adventure, day after day.'

He followed her gaze, his eyes narrowing on the photos of his childhood self. 'It wasn't anything like you would expect.'

He carried on down the hallway, naming each room in a bored monotone as they passed through.

They made their way up the sweeping staircase and Dara began to amble down the corridors more slowly behind her grumpy guide. She wanted to look at the place properly—not just power through at lightning speed.

She stopped as they passed right by a set of large double doors. She knew from the rest of the castle that it would lead to yet another private wing.

'You never said what's through this way,' she called to him as he continued to stride down the hall ahead of her.

'That one is off-limits. Keep moving.' He stopped at the top of the hall impatiently.

She frowned. They were supposed to be inspecting the entire castle in order for her to arrange the renovations. How could any area be off-limits?

'This is beginning to sound like a scene from a really lame fairy tale. Is that where the beast lives?' She chuckled, hoping to lighten the mood.

She could see his silhouette, unmoving at the end of the hall, one hand resting on a side table as he waited for her to follow him. She felt frustration bubble to the surface. He had been extremely irritable all morning, and since arriving at the castle he had stopped interacting with her completely. He clearly wasn't up to doing this job properly, but that didn't mean she wouldn't get it done.

'I need to get a look at the whole place. No exceptions.'

She turned the handle of the door to the wing slowly, watching to see his reaction. He didn't budge as the sound of the hinges creaking open echoed through the hall.

Well, he could suit himself, then, she thought stubbornly. He could stay out here in his bad mood all he wanted.

Clutching her clipboard, she threw the doors wide and continued through to the mysterious forbidden wing.

Leo stood frozen in the hallway, listening as Dara's footsteps echoed through his past. He'd told her not to go there. Of course she hadn't listened. She was hell-bent on dredging up every memory this godforsaken place had to offer.

His initial view of the castle hadn't bothered him as much as he had thought it would. After twelve years he still remembered every window, every crack in the facade. He had vowed to remain emotionless and logical. It was a building—not a demon. He would show her around in a practical fashion, get the building work arranged and then make an effort to apologise for last night.

After his meeting with Umberto, and all their talk of this place, he had found himself momentarily regretting his pursuit of Dara. His uncle's deal was tempting, but agreeing to it meant lying and double-crossing.

He shouldn't care about hurting her. He should have just taken what she had clearly been ready to offer. But something in him had stalled, and he had spent the night driving furiously up a myriad of coastal roads, then returning to the *palazzo* once he'd been sure she had gone to bed.

He turned back towards the doors she

had disappeared through. He wasn't going down there. There was only so much he could take in one day. This castle housed more than just his own cold childhood memories.

A loud bang came from down the corridor, and a woman's scream. *Damn it, Dara*, he thought angrily as he took off through to the largest wing of the castle, down the long carpeted corridor and into the grand master bedroom where his parents had once slept.

Dara stood on one of the ghostly covered chairs, her eyes darting around the floor wildly. 'Sorry, there were rats on the bed!' she squeaked, holding her battered clipboard like a shield in front of her. 'Bloody huge ones.' She shuddered.

Leo's eyes swept across to the large bed that dominated the room. A high majestic canopy flowed down from the ceiling to rest on the four-poster. His mother had imported it from Paris. He remembered her boasting about it to one of her friends. It had belonged to a queen. That had been his mother, she had always been fascinated by royalty.

The weight of long-suppressed memories was beginning to crush his self-restraint. He needed to get out of this castle now… before he lost his mind.

'I told you not to come in here,' he growled, watching as her eyes went wide. 'Get down from the damned chair. There are no rats.'

Dara lowered one foot to the floor, still anxiously scanning the perimeter of the dark room.

'There were at least three of them. They scurried off when I dropped my clipboard…' she said, her knuckles white as chalk as she held up the makeshift shield.

'I don't give a damn about rats. The place is likely infested with all kinds of vermin.'

He pinched the bridge of his nose, trying to ignore the memories threatening to engulf him. Lifeless brown eyes, staring into nothing…

'I will need to make sure that all the rooms have been cleared before we can consult the restoration contractor,' she rambled on beside him, unaware of his inner turmoil. 'Leo, are you even listening to me? We need to note all the details—'

She stepped closer and he turned to her without warning.

'Just stop with your details for once and get the *hell* out of this room.' His voice was harsh and he watched her eyes widen with shock.

'Leo... I'm sorry if I've said something to bother you.'

'I'm fine,' he gritted. 'I need to go find the housekeeper. You can finish the rest of the tour by yourself.'

He turned on his heel and strode from the room. It took all his strength not to run as if he was being chased by the ghosts that plagued his memory.

He should never have come back to this place. It made him feel things he'd vowed never to feel again. But it wasn't Dara's fault that he was on edge, and he made a mental note to make it up to her once he'd got his temper under control.

After three hours spent cataloguing every room of the *castello* Dara needed a shower.

Badly. Out of the entire estate only three bedrooms were kept open and maintained, along with the kitchen, one of the dining rooms and a downstairs salon. Every other room was closed up, its furniture sheathed in ghostly white dust covers.

Still, it was rather magical, being the only person wandering around a place filled with so much character. Leo had left the castle entirely, leaving a message with the housekeeper to tell her that they would be having dinner at six. His desertion didn't faze her. She'd enjoyed her time alone with her work. The thought of all of the possibilities that this place held made her giddy as she chose a bedroom with an en-suite bathroom and set about having a hot shower to wash off all the dust.

Weddings could be held here in any season, she mused as she towel-dried her hair into soft waves at the gilt dressing table by the bed. Outdoor summer ceremonies overlooking the cliffs…candlelit winter feasts in the ballroom. She really did adore her job, and she knew she could make this *castello* beautiful again—bring it back to life.

Not only would she be known for planning the wedding of the year, but she would also have exclusive rights to one of the most sought-after venues in the country.

Once she had dressed, in a simple black wrap dress and her trusty heels, she made her way down to the dining room for dinner.

Leo stood at the fireplace, stepping forward as she entered the room.

'Glad to see you've returned.' She breezed past him, determined not to show how his continued coldness was affecting her.

Leo helped her into one of the chairs at the end of a ridiculously long banquet table. 'I hope you're hungry? Maria has outdone herself.'

Their place settings were side by side— much more convenient than having to shout across the room to one another along the length of the table.

'This is quite intimate for a simple meal.' She poured herself a glass of wine, noticing that each of the antique candelabra had been lit around the room. The overall effect was beautiful, and strangely romantic. 'All we're missing is a violinist and I'd feel like a real aristocrat,' she joked.

'I'll make a note of that.' He smiled as Maria began serving an array of delicately prepared seafood.

The smell of lemon-drizzled prawns filled the air, to be followed by *pesce spada* and oven-roasted vegetables. Swordfish was her personal favourite since moving to Sicily.

They spoke of Dara's thoughts on the renovations, and Leo listened intently to her excited plans. By the time the house-keeper cleared their plates Dara's hunger had been well and truly satisfied.

Leo finished off his glass of wine, thanking Maria for her service and refusing dessert. They were both in favour of allowing the older woman to go home for the night after such a spectacular meal.

Leo sat forward in his seat once they were alone, his green eyes darker than usual in the muted lighting. 'I wanted to apologise for my behaviour, Dara.'

'You have no need to apologise for anything. We are both entitled to change our minds.'

'Is that what you think happened?' He shook his head. 'Dara, look at me. I haven't changed my mind about anything. Not one bit. I just felt I had coerced you into this. Had been heavy-handed.'

She felt something lift inside her, knowing he hadn't rejected her. Not that it made his treatment of her any less harsh. 'I'm a grown woman who can make her own choices, you know. I wouldn't have been willing to—you know…if it wasn't something I wanted.'

Leo laughed. 'It seems I've made a complete mess of this.'

He held her gaze for a moment before standing up.

'I want to show you the beach before it gets dark—would you walk with me?'

Dara hesitated, looking down at her shoes. 'It's October…'

'We can take ten minutes to enjoy the sunset—you won't freeze. Don't deny yourself the little pleasures in life. It's not always about the bigger picture.'

Dara followed Leo through the kitchens and down some stone steps at the back of the castle. The courtyard was growing darker by the minute as they traversed the gardens towards the cliff face.

Leo removed his shoes, leaving them at the top of the stone steps. He turned back to her, looking to where she stood poised on the top step.

'Come on, do something spontaneous for once.'

'I'm not as rigid as you seem to believe I am,' she said, and slid off her delicate heels.

Dara took his arm as they descended the stone steps to the beach below the cliffs. She felt slight terror at the height, but Leo gripped her hand tight until they set foot on the sand.

'My tutor brought me down here sometimes for science lessons.' He picked up a small stone, throwing it across to land in the water with a splash. 'He was the most uninteresting man I have ever known.'

Dara was intrigued at his sudden willingness to talk about his childhood. 'You didn't go to school?'

'The schools around here were too common for my father. He believed himself and his family far too important. I had many tutors. All in the castle.'

'That sounds rather lonely.'

'I never knew any different.' He shrugged. 'It was just the way things were.'

Dara imagined the young boy she had seen in the photographs all alone, wandering the castle grounds. 'Did your mother approve of your isolation?'

Leo walked further down the beach towards a small marina nestled into the cliff face. 'My mother didn't really have an opinion on very much.'

Dara followed closely behind him. 'You seemed quite angry when I went into her bedroom today.'

'Family history is not my favourite topic,' he said, surveying the small dock.

'I understand that.' Dara understood all too well.

She watched as Leo stepped forward onto the rickety wooden pier. There was one boat tied up to a post. Wood rotten and black in some parts, it was amazing it hadn't succumbed to the ocean already. She would imagine the weather could get pretty rough here during high tide.

Leo cleared a place on the dock so that they could sit and watch the sun sinking down into the sea.

'What about you, Dara? Any skeletons in your perfectly organised little closet?'

She shrugged. 'I suppose everyone has some event or relationship in their past that shapes their future.'

'That was a very polite way of deflecting my question.'

'I don't have some sort of deep, dark secret, if that's what you mean. My childhood was quite normal. No sob stories, no traumatic events.'

He turned to look at her briefly. 'Well, then, what made you move away from such a perfect happy life?'

'My career brought me here and I decided to stay.'

'And yet you have never replaced Mr Ex-Fiancé? Did it end badly?'

'Very few relationships end calmly and logically.' She toyed with the hem of her dress, feeling uncomfortable at the turn this conversation had taken.

'So what was it that made you decide you weren't going to marry him?' Leo asked.

She sighed, shrugging one shoulder. Clearly he wasn't going to give up on this line of questioning any time soon, so she might as well give him something. 'Dan was a very successful doctor—a highly regarded surgeon. Top of his field. He made it clear that he wanted the professional family set-up. You know…loving wife with dinner on the table, two darling children to kiss goodnight. He had all the details planned—including the name of the golden retriever we would have.'

'Sounds very detailed. A match made in heaven, I would think.'

'On paper, I suppose it was. I thought it was what I wanted. Thought it would make us both happy. But in the end I just didn't tick all of the boxes.'

'You couldn't give him the golden retriever?' Leo asked playfully.

Dara felt her breath catch in her throat,

the memory of that day in the hospital crashing down on her.

'I couldn't give him children.'

Leo's smile faded. 'And that was a problem for him?'

She nodded. 'I found out when we had been engaged for a little over a year. Three months before our wedding was planned. I had been feeling ill and I went into hospital for some tests. The doctors were beginning to worry that there was something sinister going on.'

Dara remembered her fear when nobody had been able to give her any answers for her strange symptoms. She'd been twenty-three. The doctors had never even considered that premature menopause might be the cause for her chronic headaches, insomnia, hot flushes. The day her doctor had sat her down and told her she was becoming infertile and there was no cure…

'When I told Dan he was very understanding at first. The medical mind in him made him want to know all the details and consult some colleagues. We tried to salvage what few eggs I might have left, but it was too late.'

Leo laid a hand over hers and she fought the urge to pull away. He would pity her now—just as her entire family did. Poor barren Dara and her useless body. The old self-loathing threatened to overpower her.

She stood up quickly, shaking the sand off her dress in quick sharp movements.

'What happened with your fiancé?' Leo stood too, looking at her warily, as though afraid she would run away at any moment.

'Isn't it obvious?' Dara shook her head, a harsh laugh escaping her lips. 'He wanted a wife who could procreate. It was a pretty straightforward situation.'

'He left you because of your condition? What a heartless bastard.' Leo looked furious.

Dara sighed, looking out at the red-tinged sky. Leo didn't understand how difficult things had been in the months leading up to her diagnosis. She had been ill with headaches every day, and deathly tired. And sex had been so painful they had stopped having any at all. It had felt as if every single trace of her femininity had died in the hospital that day, along with her hopes of ever being a mother.

Lying in her hospital bed, she had overheard her father speaking with Dan in hushed tones in the hallway outside. The two men who were both supposed to have loved her, talking about how she was 'barren as the desert' and what a shame it was as she was so beautiful—as if it had stained her in some way.

Leo looked appalled. 'Did this Dan treat every woman like a prize mare or was it just you?'

'He had a very clear plan for his life. We both did. I decided to offer him a chance to reconsider our relationship. It knew it wasn't easy for him to be with me all those months. I was irritable all the time, and I had virtually no interest in sex. If he'd stayed with me he would never have fathered a child the normal way.'

'Like I said— he was heartless,' Leo said plainly, looking her straight in the eyes. 'It's not your fault that nature did this to you. You should never have been made to feel inferior.'

'I was never very family orientated, but I suppose I always just presumed I would have children one day. Now that the choice has been taken from me I'm actually quite happy to focus on my career.'

She had her arms wrapped around herself. Leo felt the urge to embrace her, but decided against it. He now understood why she was so ambitious, so driven and serious. She had immersed herself in her career, moved to a new country—all in an effort to outrun her painful past. In a way they were quite similar.

This conversation had got far too deep for two people who had only met a few short days ago.

Dara looked at him, her expression one of quiet contemplation. 'I'm sorry, I should never have allowed this to get so personal.'

'Never apologise to me, Dara.' He stepped closer. 'Not for this. Don't ever let anyone think that you are less of a woman because of your condition.'

'With the way things were with Dan, I

thought I was destined to live a life of celibacy. And then you came along and all of a sudden I feel…sexual again. I almost feel normal.'

'In my experience, what we feel when we touch is far from "normal".' Leo felt arousal thrum in his veins as she nipped her teeth along her lower lip. 'I want nothing more right now than to drag you up to the nearest bed and bury myself deep inside you until you can't think.'

'Oh…' she breathed, her voice husky with desire. 'I should be appalled at such a primitive statement…'

'You're not, though—are you?' He stepped closer, moulding his body against her soft warmth. Holding her to him so that she could feel just how badly he wanted her.

'No. I want you to take me right here on this beach,' she said plainly, a smile playing on her sensual mouth.

Leo claimed her mouth in a hard kiss, any thought of gentle seduction gone from his mind. He kissed her until their breath was ragged, her lips swollen and pink.

Grabbing her by the hand, he began powering across the sand to the stone steps.

'What happened to doing it right here?' she asked breathlessly, colour high on her cheeks as they practically ran up the beach.

'I think I can manage to get you to a bed at least once. I won't have you thinking I'm a complete barbarian.'

He winked, gathering her up into his arms swiftly before she could protest.

'Nope, not a barbarian at all.' She laughed as he carried her up the steps two at a time.

CHAPTER SIX

LEO SET HER down in the middle of his bedroom, his breathing only slightly laboured from the exertion. 'There will be no stopping tonight,' he warned, as he pulled off his shirt.

She began unwrapping the tie of her dress, her hands trembling with excitement as she watched him unzip his jeans. Watching him undress, she let her hands still in their progress. Her mouth felt completely dry as she took in his smooth, muscular abs, the dusting of dark hair on his chest that trailed down his stomach in a perfect line.

'Are you just going to watch me or take off some clothes yourself?' he challenged.

'Shut up and kiss me,' she growled, throwing her hands around his neck and glorying in the feeling of having his mouth on hers again.

It wasn't enough. She moaned, running her fingertips along his shoulders, feeling the muscles bunch under her touch.

Suddenly his hands were everywhere, caressing her neck, cupping her breasts. He pulled her tight and pressed her hard against the door behind her. She felt herself held between its hard surface and his hard body and moaned again.

He undid the tie of her dress, pulling the material down her shoulders and letting it pool on the floor. She stood there, in her plain white bra and lacy thong, and gloried in the look of appreciation on his face.

Removing her bra to free her breasts, he kissed each tip briefly before running his hands down her abdomen slowly. Without warning he sank to his knees in front of her.

Dara felt her body freeze momentarily as his lips touched against the material of her underwear. She had tried this once in the past, but hadn't liked the sense of exposure it gave her. She debated pulling him up to kiss him again, only to feel his hands pulling the material swiftly to one side.

His mouth pressed against her sex—hard and hot. His tongue darted slowly between her folds, stroking against her in a rhythm so slow and firm she thought she might melt. The sensation of being kissed and licked so intimately by him was far removed from anything she had ever felt before. She didn't feel exposed…she felt worshipped.

Her orgasm built slowly, every inch of her body tightening to an almost painful peak before exploding in a spectacular release. She let herself give in to this gift he was giving her, murmuring with satisfaction as the tremors subsided.

That little noise seemed to drive him wild. He stood and twined his fingers in her hair, held her while his tongue plundered her mouth. He was greedy, his tongue like fire against her own. She could taste herself on his lips, and the erotic thought turned her on even more as she scraped her fingertips down his back.

She needed him now—before she burst

into flames. He seemed to understand her urgency. One sharp tug and her underwear was on the ground, in a pool around her feet.

His eyes closed and a deep growl sounded from his throat as she reached down to pull at his briefs. He was rock solid, so large she was amazed he didn't tear the fabric through. As her fingers closed around him she heard his deep intake of breath, a low moan. They were both breathing frantically, urgency taking them over. He removed his briefs and raised one of her thighs to wrap it around his waist.

She needed him inside her now. No more waiting. Her hips arched up to meet his, and she felt the long hard heat of his erection enter her in one deliberately slow thrust. His lips nuzzled into her neck as he retreated, then thrust again, the sensation making her shudder. He quickened the pace, grabbing her other thigh so that she was fully wrapped around him.

She understood the frantic movement of his hips. She felt the same raw greed that was consuming him. She needed more… so much more.

Her back was flattened hard against the wall as he worked magic between her thighs, and she felt the toe-curling pressure rise within her once again. His breath was heavy against her neck, his tongue tasting her and nipping her skin as she twisted her hands greedily in his hair.

All of a sudden she was pulled from the wall and carried a few steps. Expecting to be thrown down on the bed, she bit her lip as her back came in contact with the smooth surface of a wooden desk, the intimate contact between them unbroken. His eyes darkened at the look of surprise on her face as he moved within her again, this time with his hands on her breasts, his fingers on the tight peaks driving her even wilder.

'That's it…come for me again,' he purred, his eyes watching her as she writhed with every thrust.

She shook her head. It was right within her reach…she was at breaking point…she just couldn't seem to get high enough. As though reading her thoughts, he slipped one finger between their bodies, caressing her where the fire burned hottest.

Light exploded behind her eyelids as release crashed upon her. His thrusts came faster and harder, his mouth lowering to her breasts, devouring them as he sought his own release. She shattered into a million pieces just as he groaned, his hands gripping her hips as his orgasm took over.

His thrusts slowed, her own spasms eased off, and she vaguely felt the weight of his head resting upon her bare breasts. Neither of them made a sound for a moment, letting their breathing return to normal. She felt as though her body would collapse if she tried to move any time soon.

He moved to drop a kiss between her breasts before raising up to look at her. Deep green eyes seared into hers with a heat so intense it might have burnt through metal.

'I thought we might have at least made it to a bed this time,' he breathed, running his fingers slowly from her breasts to her stomach as he stood up straight. She shivered in response and he smiled. A slow, predatory smile of complete satisfaction.

Despite the molten heat still thrumming in her veins, she felt suddenly aware that she was *very* naked. She sat up on the desk and slid herself down to her feet, feeling the heat of his body press up against her. This was insane—they had barely finished and he was kissing her again, running his hands up and down her body. She had never been savoured like this before... as if her skin was irresistible.

'I can't think straight,' he growled, leaning down and pressing his forehead to hers. 'I can't stop touching you.'

They stood still for a moment, just looking at each other. Leo grabbed her by the hand and led her slowly into the en-suite bathroom. They stood in the shower stall and he turned the water on full blast, fumbling with the nozzle until the temperature adjusted from chilly to pleasantly warm.

He pulled her into his arms in one movement, the warm water cascading down over them, and Dara sighed and moulded her body to his. The sensation of their hot wet skin fused together was sinfully erotic.

He grabbed a bottle of shampoo and massaged it first into his own hair, then hers. His fingers loosened her already relaxed muscles. She hadn't thought his touch could get any more amazing. She had been wrong. His soapy hands moved over every inch of her skin, his fingers leaving a trail of fire in their wake.

His hands tilted her head back into the spray and the water rinsed the soap from her hair and body as he continued to trail soft kisses down her neck. She moved against him, feeling the smooth hot thrust of his erection slide against her stomach.

'You know, there's something I've never done…' She tried to keep her voice steady and confident as the image of what she was about to suggest flooded her senses.

'Mmm…? And what might that be?' He continued to kiss her neck, strong fingers kneading the soft flesh of her bottom as they ground against each other under the spray.

She broke the contact between them, releasing herself from his hold and meeting his eyes intensely. 'Sit down,' she commanded, gesturing to the long seat that lined the shower wall.

His brows rose but he obeyed, lowering his tall lean frame onto the seat with ease. She looked down at him and thought this had to be the single most erotic image she had ever seen. His dark wet skin was in sharp contrast with the white tiles of the shower wall. His hair was wet and curled dangerously around his features. She towered over him in this position, and felt strangely aroused by the sensation of sensual power she held over such a man.

Getting down on her knees, she moved between his legs and watched his eyes widen in surprise. She placed her hands on his thighs and felt the muscles bunch in response. She wrapped her fingers around the long hard length of him and took a moment to simply slide her hand up over the smooth silky skin.

She'd never been allowed to do this before. And the sensation felt strangely forbidden. As his breathing quickened she leaned forward and tasted him with the tip of her tongue. He arched his back in response and made a sharp hissing sound.

'Is this good for you?' she asked uncertainly.

His laugh was half choked. 'Oh, it's more than good.'

He twined his fingers through her hair, applying pressure to the back of her head as she took him in deeper. He moaned in response and she moved a little faster, rejoicing when he groaned louder.

His arms reached down and pulled her up suddenly, lifting her until she slid onto his lap with ease. She twined her fingers around his neck and felt him enter her quickly.

'Do you see what you do to me?' he groaned as she began to move over him.

Being on top gave her the same sensation of being completely in power, completely in control of their pleasure. This alone was enough to topple her over the edge. She moved her hips forward and back, moaning when he grabbed her hips greedily and began to urge her on even faster.

'Don't stop,' he murmured, running his hands over her bottom and up her back, kissing a fevered path along her neck with lips that seemed to be made of molten lava.

Dara felt her orgasm building once more, and she felt the frantic beating of his heart that signalled his own. She slowed her pace, feeling him starting to lose control. One final sweep of her hips had them both tumbling over the edge and she collapsed on top of him as the tremors racked her body.

Dara woke to an unknown sound intruding on her dreams. It took her a moment to take in her unfamiliar surroundings, and then she looked to find she was alone in the large bed.

The sheets were tangled from the events of the night before. They had made love countless times throughout the night. Leo's appetite was insatiable. The gauze curtains around the queen-size bed swayed in the breeze—she could smell oranges and salt from the surf.

She felt wickedly satisfied and smiled,

giving her hips a little wiggle as she got out of bed to look out of the windows at the waves crashing against the cliffs below the castle turrets. She wouldn't let herself regret last night. She felt happy and attractive and sensual again, and that was nothing to be ashamed of. He had given her a wonderful gift without even realising it.

As she opened the bedroom door the smell of acrid smoke burnt her nostrils and she instinctively launched into a run, bare feet clipping down the marble tiles. She reached the kitchen just in time to see Leo drop a steaming pot of coffee into the sink with a guttural oath.

'Is everything okay?' she asked, taking in the coffee grounds spilled across the counter and down onto the floor. It was as though a small child had decided to play chef.

'No, everything is *not* okay. This is the second time it's burnt,' he growled. 'Apparently Maria doesn't work until noon. What's the point in hiring a housekeeper if she's not here for breakfast?'

His brow furrowed as he emptied the

contents of the pot down the drain and peered inside the lid.

Dara stepped up beside him and peered in herself. The bottom of the steel pot was coated with a layer of thick burnt coffee grounds. He had put the coffee and the water in the wrong compartments.

'Have you ever made your own coffee?'

His frown deepened. 'It can't be that difficult, surely?'

'You really are a pampered playboy.' She chuckled, taking the ruined pot and setting it to steep in cold water.

'You seem very well rested this morning.' He smiled, stepping behind her.

'I don't see how. We didn't sleep very much.'

She tried to remain casual, unsure of what the protocol was this morning. Would he expect her to leave straight away after breakfast? There was no real need for her to stay any longer—she could arrange the renovations over the phone easily.

She felt very insecure all of a sudden.

'I've never been accused of being pampered before.' He laughed, turning her around and kissing her mouth deeply. He moaned in approval, running his hands past her waist to caress her bottom. 'Good morning…' He smiled.

'Good morning to you too.' Dara felt a little less tense, but was still unsure of her place here.

She watched as he moved to sit down lazily at the breakfast bar.

'I wouldn't get too comfortable there— I'm going to show you how to make coffee. I'm not doing it for you.'

She showed him step by step how to fill the base of the pot with fresh water and pack the coffee tight into the basket above. With a look of thoroughly male triumph he breathed in the aroma as dark liquid began to rise into the top chamber.

Dara busied herself readying a tray of food and plates to take out onto the terrace, where they sat at the outdoor breakfast table, a large canopy shielding them from the morning sun.

Leo set down two cups of steaming coffee onto the table.

'Congratulations. You have just become

self-sufficient.' She feigned applause as he stacked his plate with some of the delicious brioche.

'I have always been self-sufficient,' he argued, taking a bite of his food. 'I simply prefer to pay people to serve me my morning coffee.'

'Paying people to care for you is not the same thing as being self-sufficient. You just wind up relying on your lifestyle to keep you afloat.'

He stopped eating and leaned forward, regarding her over the rim of his coffee cup. 'What about you, Dara? Who do you rely on?'

She thought for a moment then shrugged. 'Honestly? No one. I like to feel independent, so I do most things for myself.'

'Does your family support your choice to live so far away?'

Dara took a bite of grapefruit, taking the chance to mull over his question in her mind. Her family was the most unsupportive unit she had ever known, but she wasn't about to bare her soul to him about that. She thought of her father and his stoic chauvinistic logic. If it was up to him she would be cooking breakfast for a husband and children right now, not advancing her career.

A vision of small dark-haired children at a table suddenly came to her mind. Their father was looking on indulgently. A father with suspiciously familiar green eyes. She shook her head, chasing away the thoughts. Family was not important to her. Not any more. She preferred not to dwell on things she would never have.

She looked up from her fruit and realised he was still waiting for her to answer. 'My family aren't particularly close. Maybe that's a bad thing to some people—the great Italian family mindset and all. But it fulfils me to focus on my career. My parents send a card at Christmas and birthdays. I do the same. It works for us.' She shrugged.

'I'm not judging you, believe me. I'm the last person to lecture anyone about family values. I don't even own a home.'

'Oh? I presumed you had a collection of luxury penthouse apartments dotted across the world.'

'I own plenty of real estate, of course. Paris, Barcelona, New York—you name it. Luxury apartments, mostly. But that's not the same as having somewhere you can call home.'

He sat back comfortably in his seat, looking out at the view of the ocean below them.

She was suddenly quite curious. 'If you don't own a home, then where do you live?'

'I don't live anywhere in particular. I stay wherever my work takes me. It's practical.' He finished the last of his coffee, setting the cup down on the table and sitting back again in the chair.

Dara shrugged, also looking out across the view. She sensed the matter ran a little deeper than that. A man didn't live in hotel rooms all year round just because it was 'practical'.

Leo stood up, deciding to deflect the conversation by gathering Dara into his arms.

She placed a hand on his chest, holding him away from her lips.

'Leo, what are we doing here?' she asked quietly.

'We are two adults who are about to go back upstairs to have fantastic sex for the rest of the afternoon,' he said confidently, moving the strap of her nightgown down her shoulder smoothly.

'I mean, what am *I* doing here? I have a job in Syracuse... I have clients. And you have your own company to run. This is madness.'

It *was* madness—they both knew it. But he had never felt so enthralled by an affair before. He was wealthy enough to have people run his affairs for a few days with minimum fuss while he indulged in a little leisure time. And Dara had already said that she could run her business remotely during low season.

After last night, the prospect of selling the *castello* and hurting Dara felt even more uncomfortable. But this wasn't about feelings—it was about sex, and they both knew that.

'I think we both know what we want, Dara. And I for one am prepared to take a few days away from reality to have it.'

'You want me to stay here? With you?'

'I want you in my bed for as many nights as it takes for us to tire of each other.'

He leaned down to kiss her neck, feeling his groin tighten as she moaned in response.

'I think that can be arranged,' she said breathlessly.

'I think this is my favourite deal of all.'

Leo smiled seductively, taking her by the hand and leading her back to the bedroom.

CHAPTER SEVEN

THE NEXT COUPLE of days passed in a haze of sexual fog. Most of their time was spent in the bedroom—they ventured out only for nourishment and a bout of fresh air.

The fresh air had consisted of a late-night walk on the beach, when he'd proceeded to make love to her slowly on the old wooden dock, with the sea water lapping around them.

Naturally Dara still found time to arrange some inspections for the structural work that needed to be done. And a removal team was organised for that morning, to ensure none of the antique furniture would be damaged during the building work.

Mountains of furniture now sat in the grand hall, cluttering up the space. Leo came to a stop in the hall just as a group of workmen finished carrying an elegant cherrywood vanity table down the stairs.

'What do you think you're doing with that?' he bellowed, feeling hot rage course through him at the sight of their filthy grease-smeared hands.

The men had been laughing at some private joke, but at the sound of his voice they faltered, letting one side of the table fall to the tiles with a sharp thud. Leo watched with horror as a long crack snaked through the precious glass mirror.

He felt fear grip his throat and moved with lightning-fast speed, squaring up to one of the workmen dangerously. 'Do you realise what you've done?' he shouted.

A memory clawed at his mind… Her eyes were black as night and filled with rage as she towered over him…

He barely registered Dara's hands on his shirtsleeve, pulling him back from the cowering man.

'Leo. He's just doing his job,' she pleaded, her eyes wide with worry.

He towered over her. '*Nothing* is to be moved from the master rooms—you hear me? Leave it the way it is or this whole thing is over.'

She stood back from him, confusion and hurt clouding her eyes. 'But the work covers the whole castle, Leo. All this furniture has been ruined with water damage…it's worthless now.'

It had always been worthless to him, he thought harshly, remembering his mother's reflection in the shiny glass. Everything about that room was toxic.

But it needed to be left alone or it would seep out and drag him under all over again.

'Just put it back,' he gritted, turning on his heel and stalking out through the door.

His breath came in deep bursts as he strode away from the courtyard. The cypress trees shielded him from the sun as he followed the stone path down the side of the hill. This whole place was one big black spot in his memory—a black hole of loneliness and despair. Dara thought he hated it because of the memory of death. She didn't understand that the memories of life could be far worse.

He didn't know where he was going until

he heard the crunch of stone disappear and realised he was heading across the formal gardens to the large stone family crypt. The structure was an original part of the castle, restored by his grandfather in an effort to make some sort of tradition for his family. He needed to go in—needed to remind himself of who he was. He wasn't that lonely boy any more.

His feet echoed on the marble steps as he reached the tall black iron-clad door. It was never locked, always open for mourners to come and pay their respects. Resting his fingers on the cold metal, he took a deep breath and pushed.

The door swung forward easily, cold air rushing forward like the fingers of death on his face. And just like that he was engulfed by the dark damp smell of his childhood.

'Leonardo, you must learn to be silent,' she had commanded him, pushing her soft hand against his head until he was inside the darkness of the bad place.

He'd looked up at his mother's beautiful face, at green eyes just like his own, thick dark curls bathed in light from the outside world. She'd leaned down to kiss him on the forehead lightly, her fingers still clutching his shirt collar, reminding him of her power. He'd begged her to forgive him, told her he hadn't meant to come into her room, hadn't meant to speak out loud. He had forgotten Mamma's rule again.

She'd shaken her head, pushing him back. 'Silence, *piccolo mio*. When you learn to be silent Mamma will let you come out.'

The door had closed with a bang, the echo bouncing off the marble tombs that lined the walls. He'd smacked his hands over his ears until the vibrations had stopped. Then there had been nothing. Only darkness so thick and black it had been as if light had never existed.

He'd sat down against the cold stone graves where his ancestors' dead bodies nestled until the cold had seeped into his bones...

The breath returned to his lungs with a shuddering gasp and he felt a warm hand on his shoulder. He looked up to see Dara, the sun glowing in her blonde hair through the open doorway of the crypt. He became aware that he was hunched, sitting against the tomb nearest the door. How long had he sat here? And how much had she seen?

He stood up, wiping the dust from his jeans with quick sharp smacks, avoiding her eyes as he tried to get his heartbeat back under control.

'Are you okay?' She looked concerned, her brow marred by a thin line of worry.

'I'm fine,' he gritted.

'You're sweating.' She reached a hand out to touch his forehead.

'Damn it, Dara, I said I'm fine.'

He grabbed her hand, holding on to the warm skin and feeling its silky heat seep into him. Touching her skin seemed to remind him that his words were true. He was a grown man, and ghosts had no power over him.

He grasped her hand tightly and steered her out of his nightmare and into the light of the gardens.

'Where are we going?' she asked breathlessly as they powered through the overgrown gardens towards the low stone wall of the castle perimeter.

'I want to show you something.'

He led them down 'his' path—the path he had always taken as a young boy. The smell of the sea filled his nostrils, loosening the tight pain in his chest. The rocks were tall and smooth as they descended the swift decline from the castle to the sea. His footsteps were steady and he held her hand tight, gripping her waist at times so she wouldn't fall. The afternoon wind whipped around them as the weather took an unseasonably stormy turn.

The last of the smooth rocks ended sharply and he jumped down onto the sand of the beach, holding her by the waist and lowering her safely. His fortress still lay nestled in the rocks. A safe, sturdy structure made from stone and mortar. He pushed the door, feeling the hinges creak and groan as they gave way. The roof and walls were still intact—the water hadn't yet claimed his little haven.

'What *is* this place?' Dara asked, her

voice breathless from their climb down, her blonde hair wild around her face.

The small square room had stone floors and tiny latticed windows. He vaguely remembered the walls had been painted a dull white, but now years of damp had rendered them almost black in some places.

'It was used as a boathouse at one time, back when my father still lived here. One day I was running away and I found it. It became my own little castle.' He smiled at the memory.

'Did you run away very often?' She frowned.

'Oh, all the time. I would plan my escape in detail, pack a suitcase and food and take off.'

He walked across to the small grimy window, looking out at the wild stormy sea outside.

'I used to imagine I was a pirate, waiting for my ship to come and rescue me from a desert island. It varied, really, the mind of a boy is fickle. One day a pirate, the next day a dragon-slayer. I never could choose just one.'

She smiled, wrapping her arms around herself in the chill. 'That sounds very exciting. Did you always return home after these little adventures?'

'A boy runs out of food very quickly when he's slaying dragons, Dara.'

'Didn't your mother ever wonder where you were?'

'No. Never. I rarely saw her, you see. This was my castle, and her bedroom was hers. Our paths rarely crossed.' He pushed away the memories.

'Is that why you don't want her room disturbed? Because it was her place?'

Leo crossed back to where Dara stood, shivering in the doorway.

'I don't want to talk about ghosts any more.' He smiled, sliding his hands up and down her soft skin, warming her. 'In my castle we play games until we're forced to go back for food.'

She raised an eyebrow. 'Adults don't play games, Leo.'

'Ah, my poor, serious Dara, I beg to differ.' He leaned in, biting softly into the sensitive skin of her earlobe.

'You can't mean…?' She gasped. 'In here? But it's freezing cold.'

'I promise we can find ways to keep warm.'

Dara lay boneless and relaxed, listening to the sound of Leo's breathing return to normal. His eyes were closed but she could feel the tension slowly returning to his body as he came down from the glow of their lovemaking.

This time seemed to have been more intense than before, with a pile of nets and blankets providing a makeshift bed for their heated bodies. As attentive and sensual as he had been, he hadn't been able to shake the shadows from his eyes. It was as though some unknown force was still there and he was running, using the intense pleasure between them to get away from it.

She sat up on her elbows, looking down at his tousled curls against her bare stomach. 'Tell me what happened back there?' she asked gently.

His voice rumbled against her skin. 'You

mean when I lay you down and told you I would be the dragon this time?'

'Be serious for once, would you? You were sitting in that crypt with a look of terror on your face, Leo. It scared me.'

'I'm a grown man, Dara—' He protested, sitting up on the makeshift bed and grabbing his jeans from the crumpled pile of clothes on the dusty stone floor.

She sat up too, placing a hand on his shoulder, stopping him from moving away from her. 'Even grown men have nightmares.'

He laughed. 'Nightmares would have made my childhood a little more entertaining. As you can see, I suffered from boredom.'

'Children don't run away from home because they're bored.'

He sighed. Standing up, he walked over to a small chest of trinkets, his jeans draped low on his hips.

'My mother liked silence.' He spoke in a monotone, tracing his finger along the silver lid of the box. 'She would fly into a rage whenever her peace was disturbed.

I imagine it had something to do with the multitude of medication she took daily. Anyway, on occasion a young boy likes to make noise. When I got too loud she would send me there for quiet time.'

'To the crypt?' Dara felt shock pour into her veins. She remembered how pale and terrified he had looked, pushed tight against the marble wall.

'I don't know when I realised there was something wrong with her,' he continued. 'She would be fine some days, and then others...she just wasn't. I was maybe five or six when she first put me in there. I lost my first tooth and I ran to her room to tell her. I forgot myself. It seemed like I was in that place for hours before she let me out.'

Dara felt tears choke her throat. How could a mother be so cruel to her own son? His reaction when the men had dropped the table suddenly made sense—he was used to being punished for touching anything in that room. He was used to being kept out. She sat up, forcing herself not to cry for fear he would stop.

He kept talking in that monotone, turning the trinkets over in his hands one by one.

'When I was twelve she came to find me one day. It had been months since the last episode. I had learned not to speak to her or provoke her. I had learned to be silent. She was in a blind rage—kept calling me Vittorio. Apparently I was beginning to resemble my father a little too strongly. I wouldn't go to the crypt that time. She never physically hurt me so I knew she couldn't make me go. I just remained silent until she walked away.'

'It sounds like you were forced to grow up much too soon.'

'I thought I had learned how to keep myself safe. How to keep her happy. But I woke up that night and she was trying to set my bedroom on fire.'

Dara gasped, her breath stilling in her throat.

He turned to face her, his eyes grim and lined. 'Nobody was hurt. The housekeeper had been awake and she heard my shouts. She and her husband put out the fire before it could spread too far. It was finally enough for my father to fly home from his business to take me and put me in a boarding school in Sienna.'

'What did he do with your mother?'

'She stayed here. The housekeeper knew how to keep it quiet. Father ordered more medication to help her sleep. He said she suffered with her nerves. I didn't see her for six months after that night.'

Leo shook his head. Running his fingers through his hair, he walked across to the window, staring out into the distance.

'She continued in her cycle of madness for years after that. I'd spend Christmas and summer with my father. He would bring me to see her occasionally, but she never spoke to me. I sometimes wondered why we even bothered. Boarding school changed me—I became rebellious and loud, and going back to the castle would make me feel like I was suffocating. Home became a distant nightmare. A few weeks before my eighteenth birthday I got accepted into Oxford in England. My father was determined his future CEO would get the best education. I don't know what possessed me to travel down to see her. I felt like maybe if she knew I was leaving the country I might get some sort of reaction. When I got here the castle was empty. I'll never forget the silence.'

Dara could tell by his posture that this was difficult for him. She wanted to tell him that it was fine, that he didn't have to tell her any more.

'I went to her room and she was lying on the bed wearing her best dress. I remember thinking she looked like Sleeping Beauty. I didn't touch her. I just knew. There is a certain heaviness to the air when you're in the presence of death.'

Dara covered her mouth with her hands, tears welling up in her eyes.

'She had been there for more than a day—just lying there on the bed. A week's worth of sleeping pills in her stomach. All of the staff had been sent away in one of her rages. They'd tried to call my father but he was on a yacht somewhere with one of his mistresses.'

Dara stood up and walked over to him,

touching his shoulder to find he was deathly cold. 'There was nothing you could have done. Mental illness is not something that can be cured by a son's love.'

'I don't remember feeling anything towards my mother other than fear. From six years old I knew that she was ill. I'd learned to adapt. And the day of her funeral, standing there and watching them slide her casket into the tomb...' He turned to look at her, genuine anguish hardening his features. 'I honestly felt like a dead weight had been lifted from my shoulders. There was always a fear in me—even after I went away to school. I always feared she would come back for me. She truly hated me. And as I looked into my father's eyes I saw that exact same relief and I knew she had been right. I was exactly like him.'

'Leo, your mother was ill. People in that kind of mental state can see things very differently to reality.'

'When the ceremony was over I watched him finish off his cigar and mash it into the ground outside the crypt. I felt something bubble up inside of me like never before. I had always strived to be the best, to get his approval. I'd always wanted him to notice me. *He* wasn't ill—he didn't have any excuse for his behaviour. I walked up to him and asked him why he never did anything to help her. He shook his head and said he couldn't control her personality. She was weak and had brought shame on our family name. By keeping it secret he'd spared her a lot of embarrassment. So I punched him square in the jaw and walked away. I decided that I might *look* like him but I would never be as heartless as he was.'

'So that's why you sold his company? Revenge?'

'Childish, maybe.' He shrugged, sitting down behind her and pulling her back against his chest.

'It wasn't childish. He didn't deserve your respect, Leo.'

Dara felt his warmth against her back, this marvellous man who had opened her eyes to so many things. He lived life to the fullest and disregarded the rules in order to escape all of this. Underneath the charming bad boy was someone who just wanted to be cared about.

The thought was almost too much to bear. She was beginning to care for him too much, and the feeling scared her. Knowing that he was just as damaged as she was made it harder to think of their relationship as it was. This new closeness between them was complicating things, tangling up her emotions in knots.

Leo held Dara in his arms and attempted to process the feelings trying to burst through his chest. He was thirty years old and this was the first time he had ever spoken about his upbringing to anybody. What was it about this woman that had made him want to lay himself bare?

His past was something that had always been buried in a deep crevice of his mind, filled with shame and confusion. But now, after saying it all out loud and hearing her say he was normal… He felt lighter than he had in years. The memories of fear were suddenly just that—old memories.

For the first time he felt entirely present in the moment, in this boathouse, with this woman in his arms. He felt as if he could stay still with her and not feel afraid. As if this was a safe place to stay for a little while—maybe even longer.

Later that night Leo stood in the doorway of the master bedroom while Dara slept soundly. When the call from his Paris club had awoken him he had debated on whether to wake her. But after another night of marathon lovemaking he'd decided to let her sleep. She had been working hard on the *castello* by day and spending each night in his bed. She deserved some quality sleep.

The Platinum club in Paris had got into some legal difficulty with licensing, and he was required there before midday to meet with his team of advisers. The jet was ready and he needed to leave as soon as possible. The realisation that he didn't want to leave made him all the more intent to go. He needed some head space to process the events of the past few weeks.

For so long he had been someone who avoided emotional entanglements and kept his affairs at a distance. He had bared far too much to her yesterday. She had every right to call time on whatever it was that they were doing. She hadn't signed up for a no-strings fling with an emotional wreck.

Dara's eyes fluttered open just as he moved to walk out through the door.

'Leo—where are you going?'

'Paris. I have some business to attend to.'

He fought the urge to climb back into bed with her. The thought of a morning on a plane followed by an afternoon in a courthouse was hardly a fair trade.

'Will you be gone long?' She moved the covers teasingly close to her nipples, smiling like the wicked temptress she had become.

'I'll be back as soon as my business is done. You have work to complete here too.'

Leo paused, considering his words carefully as she sat up on the bed.

'It's time we started wrapping up this deal,' he said finally, seeing the look of confusion on her face.

'Is there something wrong?' she asked.

'I'm a very busy man, Dara.' He moved towards the door. 'We'll talk when I return.'

* * *

Dara watched as Leo's car disappeared down the drive and felt her heart sink in her chest. This wasn't meant to happen. She sat down on the veranda, watching as the sun started to rise over the waves, orange and red mixing in with the mirror-like calmness of the water. He'd said this was just fun—two adults enjoying themselves and burning out an attraction.

When had it become more than that?

He knew she couldn't give him any sort of future. She had told him she was a lost cause. It would be just like her to get the idea into her head that he felt something more just because they had shared their life histories. She had spent the past five years convincing herself that she was happy alone, and she had almost begun to believe it. Now, after only a week with Leo, she knew just what she had been denying herself.

Angrily, she stood up and got dressed.

Perhaps he pitied her because of her condition. Maybe it was out of some misplaced sense of chivalry that he had stayed so long. She didn't truly want more, did she? He would never be happy with her. He was a Sicilian—it was in his blood to want children. He had never said otherwise. Sure, he lived a bachelor lifestyle now, but some time in the future he would settle down and start a family of his own. At least he had the choice.

The thought of him with another woman made her throat well up with emotion. When had she begun thinking of him as hers?

She spent the morning busily inspecting the repair work in the dining hall. All traces of water damage were gone, and the walls had been painted a burnished orange, true to the original style. She gazed up at the newly polished wooden beams on the ceiling, remembering how they had looked when they'd first arrived.

It was hard to believe it had been little more than a week since she had been thrown into Leo's world. She missed him already, and he had only been gone a few short hours.

Her thoughts were interrupted by the sound of a car coming up the driveway. He couldn't have made it all the way to Paris and back already. She got to the door just as an unfamiliar silver sports car came to a stop in the courtyard.

Umberto Lucchesi stepped out of his car, a warm smile on his face as he embraced her. 'Dara, so nice to see you again.'

'Leo isn't here, I'm afraid. He's been called away for the day on urgent matters.'

'Actually, I'm here to see you.' He smiled, stepping back to look up at the facade of the ancient *castello*. 'Don't look so worried. I simply wanted to come here and explain myself to you.'

Dara frowned. 'Explain yourself? About what?'

'Well, I presume Leo has told you he will soon be selling the castle to me?'

Dara felt the betrayal hit her like a gunshot. Her hands dropped to her sides as she took in Umberto's words.

'No, he hasn't mentioned it.' She spoke as steadily as she could.

'Yes, the deal was made in Palermo. I'm

sure you know that the *castello* originally belonged to my family?'

Dara nodded, trying to follow his words, but the knowledge that the deal had been done in Palermo cut her even deeper. He had known for days. He had known that he was going to tear her life apart and yet he'd still gone ahead and seduced her anyway.

Hot tears threatened to overflow in her eyes. A lump of emotion was forming in her chest.

'Did he send you here to tell me?' she asked quietly, trying and failing to conceal the tremor in her voice.

Umberto shook his head. 'Look, I don't want to get in between whatever is going on with you and my nephew. I just want to make sure that you know that the Lucchesi Group will be happy to fulfil this contract of yours with Miss Palmer once the *castello* is under our brand.'

'With all due respect, I've just found out that my contract is null and void. I don't think I'll be handing it over to you.'

'I'm not suggesting that. I can see you've been caught off guard, here, so I will leave

you to gather your thoughts. Come and
have lunch at the resort tomorrow and we
can talk further.'

Dara barely registered the older man getting into his car and leaving. She sat down
on one of the marble benches at the edge
of the courtyard, feeling her control finally
tearing to shreds around her. Tears flowed
down her cheeks onto her lap.

CHAPTER EIGHT

LEO WALKED INTO the main lobby of his uncle's Syracuse resort. The old man had been very cryptic about meeting him there.

After spending two full days in Paris, thinking, he had made a decision to end his business with his uncle before returning to Monterocca.

Dara was the only reason he had gone back to his childhood home. It was because of her that he had faced his demons and let go of the darkness he'd carried around with him since his mother's death. His feelings for her were intense and new, but what they had uncovered at the *castello* together was worth ten times more than any deal.

Umberto descended the main stairs and Leo raised his hand to greet his uncle—but froze as he noted the beautiful blonde step out from behind him. As he watched, Dara shook hands with Umberto, her face a polite mask of professional gratitude.

She turned and saw him just as he reached the foot of the staircase. Her features tightened and she turned away, thanking Umberto again before walking in the opposite direction.

Leo felt as though a train had just run him over. He froze in place, watching her walk away, before his brain caught up.

Umberto clapped him hard on the back, taking his hand in greeting.

'Glad to see you could make time for me, boy,' he said. 'We've had a slight change of plan with the resort, so I'm pushing the contracts through today.'

Leo moved to follow Dara across the lobby—only to have his uncle stop him.

'I won't have a scene here, Valente,' he warned.

'What is she doing here?' Leo gritted.

'Miss Devlin has accepted my offer of employment.'

'You callous bastard,' Leo breathed, seeing red haze his vision. 'You did this to convince me to sell the *castello*?'

'You have been dodging my phone calls all week. I felt like you needed some incentive. But apart from that the girl has a contract with Portia Palmer. A household name at my newest boutique hotel is an opportunity too good to miss. I wanted to make sure we were all on the same page.'

'You wanted to remove any potential roadblocks!'

Umberto shrugged. 'Leo, this is how real business is conducted. If you want in on my development then you've got to grow a thicker skin.'

'I'd much rather have a conscience.'

Leo turned and strode across the lobby in pursuit of Dara. He caught up with her just as she turned down the hallway to the business suites.

She turned to face him and he noted the telltale smudges under her eyes. She looked as if she hadn't slept or eaten in days. Like a woman who had been betrayed.

'There's nothing left to say, Leo.'

'Oh, I think there's plenty left to say.'

He spoke calmly, belying the anger coursing through him. He opened the door of an empty conference room, motioning for her to step inside.

Dara moved away from him to the head of the conference table, her hands resting on a high-backed leather chair.

Leo shut the door, turning to stare down at her. 'You have made a monumental leap of faith, trusting that snake without speaking to me first.'

'He told me that he was going to allow your investment deal in return for the sale of the *castello*—was that a lie?' She crossed her arms, hurt evident in the shiny brightness of her eyes.

Leo felt hot shame course through him at being the cause of her anger. 'I did not agree to anything.'

'But you were going to.' She was so certain in her statement.

Would she believe him if he said he'd come here today to say no to the deal? That he wanted to keep the castle?

He no longer associated Castello Bellamo with darkness and fear. Now it was filled with memories of warm soft skin and hot passion.

Dara continued, making a show of closing the clasp on her small handbag. 'I mean, why would you walk away from a million-euro deal for a small-time wedding planner you're just having a fling with? We're both adults here, Leo. We knew what this was. And to be honest I don't blame you. It's better this way. Lucchesi has promised me my own division here, so I'll be my own boss. My company would have been ruined anyway. This way I'll still get to plan the Palmer wedding. I'll be fine.'

'I came here today to tell my uncle that I was backing out of the deal. That I wanted to keep the *castello* after all.'

'Why on earth would you do that?'

'Because for the past week I've been more honest and real than I've ever been before. You crashed into my life and forced me to revisit a past I never wanted to think about again. Do you have any idea what that feels like for someone like me?' He shook his head, pacing to the end of the room. 'And now you're telling me that Umberto just had to tell you I was selling the castle and you jumped ship?'

'In light of your sudden change in behaviour, it wasn't so hard to believe. Taking a position here is a secure logical move for me.'

'Screw logic!' he bellowed, turning back towards her and slamming his hand down on the conference table. 'You're so willing to just hand over that wedding contract? To give it up without a fight? What happened to the woman who climbed up a building to fight for her career?'

'I have no other choice.'

'You *always* have a choice, Dara. No one has a gun to your head. You want to know what I think? I think you're scared. You feel it too—whatever this thing is between us. And running away at the first sign of danger is easier than staying around to risk getting hurt.'

Dara stared at the man standing before her. She took a deep breath, trying to calm the chaotic thump of her heart.

Leo walked around the table to stand before her. 'You can keep pushing me away with logic and business but I know that's all a front.'

He leisurely brushed a wisp of hair from her face, making her shiver in response.

Dara stiffened, taking a quick step back from him. 'Leo…this was just sex.' Her voice was almost a whisper, the emotion in her throat making it hard for her to form words. 'Nothing more.'

She shook her head, looking out of the window to the bay below. How could she look at him when he had just offered her more and she was throwing it back in his face? She was showing her love for him by making this decision. By letting him see that this was just a week of madness. He would never be happy with a woman like her. He deserved someone whole. Someone better.

Leo stood up straight, taking a step away from her. 'Well, it's clear you've made your choice.'

Dara remained silent as he walked towards the door, pausing to look back at her. For a moment she thought he might say something else. She didn't know if she could take much more before she broke down completely. To her relief he turned and walked away without another word.

She waited until she heard his footsteps disappear before she let the tears come. The emotion of the past twenty minutes had left her gutted inside. She felt physically ill. He would be back to his old lifestyle by tomorrow. She had no doubt. Men like Leo Valente didn't brood over women. They moved swiftly on to the next willing partner.

She remembered that day in the boathouse—him laying his past out in front of her. She had seen through the playboy facade to the man underneath. Did she honestly think he was capable of such deceit or had she jumped the gun in leaving the *castello* so quickly to escape her own feelings? Maybe things would have been different if she had waited for him to explain first.

Wiping the tears from her face, she shook her head with finality. What was done was done.

She wasn't sure she would ever recover from Leo Valente. She wasn't sure she even wanted to.

Dara had thought the week since their last encounter had been difficult. But nothing compared to knowing that Leo would be in the building today, to finalise the contract for his investment in his uncle's development. She half expected to look up from her desk and see him in her doorway, all charming smiles and smooth talk. She almost hoped to see him.

Her decision to hand over the planning of Umberto's celebration dinner tonight had been made out of self-preservation. She couldn't stand to see the hurt in Leo's eyes one more time. Or, worse, to see that he had brought some leggy beauty as his date. Even the thought made her knuckles clench.

She mentally chastised herself. That was ridiculous. She had no claim on him now. She'd never even had one to begin with. And she had forfeited any rights she might have had when she'd walked away from him.

The memory of his words sent a fresh knot of emotion to her throat. *'You always have a choice, Dara.'*

'What are you doing up here? The dinner starts in twenty minutes.'

Umberto Lucchesi stood in the doorway of Dara's office, a glass of champagne in his hand.

'I don't think it would be appropriate for me to attend this evening. Considering my recent history with Mr Valente.'

'Leo won't be here this evening. Tonight is a good time for me to introduce you to the Lucchesi Group family. To celebrate the deal of the century.'

'I thought he was signing the contract today?'

'He has postponed it once again. Said he was otherwise engaged. It is merely a technicality,' the older man scoffed.

Dara felt her lips tighten at the thought of what *otherwise engaged* might mean. 'If the deal is not completely signed, why are you celebrating?'

'Among Sicilian businessmen a spoken agreement is taken just as seriously as a written contract. I will have the contract sent over to the *castello* tomorrow—he can sign it then. Tonight we celebrate.'

Then knowledge that Leo was still in Monterocca had caught her off-guard. She'd thought he would be back to jet-setting around the world by now. Knowing he was in the castle…in the place where they had shared so much… She wondered if his reluctance to leave was about business or of a more sentimental nature.

The older man continued to ramble on. 'No one is truly surprised that the castle is to be mine once more. It's just as it should always have been. Out of the hands of those traitors.' He spoke almost to himself.

'It was never yours,' Dara said quietly, and watched the man freeze and regard her through narrowed eyes.

'That *castello* belonged to my mother—and all the land that goes with it. It is mine by blood. It does not belong to some disrespectful Valente.'

Dara stood up, feeling her temper snap. 'Don't you *dare* speak about the man I love that way.'

'You forget your place here, Dara. You are my employee now, not his. Your loyalty is to me.'

'I'm beginning to realise that I've made a mistake. You are a spiteful, mean old man.'

Venom spat from every hard line on his ravaged face as he stared her down. 'Portia Palmer's wedding is contracted to me now. You walk away and you lose your client and all of your hard work for nothing.'

'It wasn't for nothing.'

Dara smiled to herself. It wasn't for nothing at all. It was for the biggest something she had ever experienced.

She grabbed her coat and bag, sidestepping Umberto Lucchesi in the doorway. Even if Leo turned her away—even if she had missed her chance—she still had to try.

Dara pulled up outside Castello Bellamo and breathed in the familiar scent of sea and oranges.

The front door opened and Maria came running out.

'I thought it was you!' She embraced her

in a warm hug. 'I told him you would come back—I told him—'

'Is he here?' Dara interrupted, the urgent need to speak with Leo overtaking her good manners.

'He's been down at the pier all day.' She smiled, warmth in her eyes. 'He needs a woman like you, Dara. You are a kind soul.'

Dara felt her eyes well up. She had probably done too much damage to expect forgiveness, but she had to at least try.

The stone steps down to the beach gave her just enough time to plan a speech in her head. But all of that went to mush when she was only a few steps away.

He had his back to her, his attention focused on a piece of wood he was repairing on the pier. He wore jeans low on his hips…his white T-shirt was torn and covered with dirt.

He turned and saw her, their eyes meeting across the short expanse of sand between them. Dara steeled her reserve and walked closer to the small wooden pier, aware of his gaze on her the whole time.

'I didn't realise you were so handy,' she said, taking in the array of tools set out alongside him.

'Hello to you too, Dara.' His face was guarded, his expression unreadable as he stepped down from his perch and wiped his hands on a nearby towel. 'My uncle sent you, I suppose?'

'Nobody sent me. I'm here because I want to be.'

'I'm honoured.' He laughed, kicking a few rocks off the polished wood with a thump.

'Please, no jokes.' Dara felt queasy with nerves, and it must have shown on her face because his expression suddenly turned deathly serious.

'Is something wrong? Is he treating you badly?'

He walked towards her.

'No, nothing dramatic like that.'

'What, then?' He met her gaze intently.

'I've missed you,' she whispered, softly placing one hand against his chest.

He looked down at her, and for a split second she imagined he might kiss her. But then he stepped away, putting distance between them. She felt her heart thump uncomfortably.

'I suppose I deserve that,' she said quietly.

'You travelled all this way just to tell me that?'

'No. I came to tell you not to sell the *castello* to Umberto Lucchesi. I've realised that I made a mistake. That you were only selling it for me now. And I'd be the reason that such a beautiful place gets exploited by that man.'

'You decided all that today—when the contract is as good as signed? Again, your timing is impeccable, Dara. What does your new boss have to say about all this?'

'It doesn't matter because I quit.'

Leo's eyes narrowed. 'Dara, please tell me that you retained your rights to the Palmer contract?'

'I didn't. The contract goes to Lucchesi. But the *castello* doesn't have to.' She took a deep breath, stepping closer to him. 'What you said about finding your home here… That means so much more to me than some celebrity wedding. I want you to be happy. I want you to have this beautiful castle and a family of your own. You deserve happiness.'

'It sounds suspiciously like you care about me…'

'I *do* care about you. I love you for sacrificing your happiness for mine, but I just couldn't live with myself if I'd let you do it.'

'Dara…' He stepped closer, reaching for her, but she held back, knowing that if he touched her she would just implode completely.

'I have never felt happier than during the time I spent here with you,' she whispered. 'I'll treasure the memory, but it's best that we both draw a line under it and carry on with our separate lives. You see, someone like me—'

'I'm going to stop you there.'

His mouth was soft on hers, his lips tasting her slowly and deliberately. She reached up and drew him closer, unable to control the raw emotion sweeping through her. This might be the last time she ever kissed him, so she needed to savour every moment.

She felt his shock as she deepened the kiss, controlling it with an urgency she had never felt before. She pressed close, so that their bodies were completely in contact. She could feel his heart beating frantically against her hand.

He was the one to break the kiss. He held her at arm's length, a slow smile spreading across his face.

'I forget what I was saying…' she mumbled, pressing a hand to her swollen lips.

'You were about to tell me that you're no good for me because you can't give me children and I deserve a complete woman. Or something else ridiculous along those lines, I imagine.'

'Right. Well, now you've taken the power out of my argument by pre-empting me.' She laughed weakly.

'There was no power there to begin with, because that's a load of lies and you know it.'

Dara began to argue but he stepped closer, wrapping his arm tighter around her waist.

'Do I have to kiss you again?' he warned.

'I love you for who you are—not how many children you can bear for me. I want to build a life with you, Dara. For us to laugh together and travel together and come home together after a hard day's work and argue over who does the dishes.'

'You are far too pampered to *ever* wash your own dishes.'

'That's true.' He laughed.

'I'm sorry I almost ruined this. I'm so used to feeling like I'm not enough. The thought that you could ever be content with just me is terrifying. And even more terrifying is that when you call me perfect… I almost start to believe it myself.'

'I will call you perfect every day until you believe it. Because that's what you are.'

'I love you,' she whispered.

'*Dio*, it took you long enough to realise it.'

He laughed into her neck, nuzzling the skin gently.

EPILOGUE

LEO WAITED IMPATIENTLY by the entrance of the *castello*. The final toasts had just been made in the marquee and the wedding guests were settling in for a night of dancing and celebrations. The June sun had been strong all day, leaving the night air balmy and the sea calm.

It had all gone off without a hitch—Dara had made sure of that. He spied her finally exiting the tent, still not a blonde hair out of place. Seeing her in action today, planning the pivotal wedding of her career, made the past eight months of stress worthwhile.

Portia Palmer had proved a much more demanding bride than the Lucchesi Group could manage, so when the *castello* sale had been cancelled Umberto had been more than happy to pass the actress on to a more capable wedding planner.

Dara had risen to the challenge with gusto, and once word had got out that she was Portia's wedding planner the requests had starting pouring in. She already had the next year booked solid, and the summer so far had included events for politicians, television personalities and minor British royalty. She was a sensation.

But, as much as their careers had kept them busy, they still found time for each other. This weekend marked the start of a two-week vacation he had been planning for weeks. It began tonight.

'There you are.' She breezed up to him, planting a kiss on his lips. 'You disappeared after dinner.'

'I have a surprise. Can I steal you away now, or are you still on headset duty?'

She touched the small black device that was clipped to her earlobe. 'I'm officially off the clock. The team have it from here.'

'Excellent.' He unclipped the earpiece

and unceremoniously threw it over her shoulder.

'Leo! That thing cost money, you know. My company's not exactly hitting the billion-euro mark just yet.'

He laughed, pulling her by the hand inside the castle and up to the master suite.

'You know, if you were that eager to take me to bed you should have just asked.' She smiled seductively, pulling at his tie.

'Not yet—first the surprise.'

'So mysterious…' she mused, following him out onto the balcony.

On cue, the sky was filled with an eruption of colour. Bursts of red and blue reflected in the bay.

'Oh, Leo, it's beautiful,' she mused. 'Portia will be so pleased. What a wonderful way to end the night.'

'I wanted to make this magical for *you*. This moment. It's been something I've been waiting to do for quite a while now.'

Dara gasped as he pulled out a small box from his pocket, knowing what was inside.

'You say I'm impulsive, but I bought this

ring the day I went to Paris. I knew even then.'

He opened the box to reveal a spectacular vintage sapphire, handpicked by himself. Something with history and class.

'You were so sure I would say yes?' she teased.

'Well, I suppose I could always take it back…' He closed the box, putting it back in his pocket.

Dara placed one hand on her hip. 'You see, I was planning on asking *you* to marry *me*. You've totally ruined the surprise now.' She tried not to smile, but failed, grinning widely.

Leo placed the ring on her left finger— a perfect fit.

'I can't wait to call you my husband. How would you like to elope to somewhere exotic?'

'No big white wedding? I thought you would want to plan a festival of extravagance for your own.'

Dara shook her head, gazing up at him with tears in her eyes. 'It doesn't matter where or when, as long as I become your wife. All I will ever want is right here in front of me.'

He leaned down and captured her mouth in a kiss that promised for ever. His perfect Dara…his home.

* * * * *

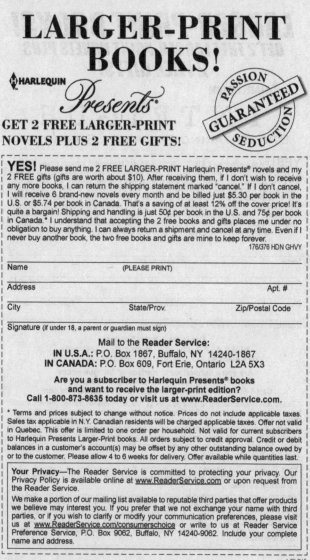

LARGER-PRINT BOOKS!

HARLEQUIN

Presents

GET 2 FREE LARGER-PRINT NOVELS PLUS 2 FREE GIFTS!

PASSION GUARANTEED SEDUCTION

YES! Please send me 2 FREE LARGER-PRINT Harlequin Presents® novels and my 2 FREE gifts (gifts are worth about $10). After receiving them, if I don't wish to receive any more books, I can return the shipping statement marked "cancel." If I don't cancel, I will receive 6 brand-new novels every month and be billed just $5.30 per book in the U.S. or $5.74 per book in Canada. That's a saving of at least 12% off the cover price! It's quite a bargain! Shipping and handling is just 50¢ per book in the U.S. and 75¢ per book in Canada.* I understand that accepting the 2 free books and gifts places me under no obligation to buy anything. I can always return a shipment and cancel at any time. Even if I never buy another book, the two free books and gifts are mine to keep forever.

176/376 HDN GHVY

Name _____ (PLEASE PRINT)

Address _____ Apt. #

City _____ State/Prov. _____ Zip/Postal Code

Signature (if under 18, a parent or guardian must sign)

Mail to the **Reader Service:**
IN U.S.A.: P.O. Box 1867, Buffalo, NY 14240-1867
IN CANADA: P.O. Box 609, Fort Erie, Ontario L2A 5X3

**Are you a subscriber to Harlequin Presents® books and want to receive the larger-print edition?
Call 1-800-873-8635 today or visit us at www.ReaderService.com.**

* Terms and prices subject to change without notice. Prices do not include applicable taxes. Sales tax applicable in N.Y. Canadian residents will be charged applicable taxes. Offer not valid in Quebec. This offer is limited to one order per household. Not valid for current subscribers to Harlequin Presents Larger-Print books. All orders subject to credit approval. Credit or debit balances in a customer's account(s) may be offset by any other outstanding balance owed by or to the customer. Please allow 4 to 6 weeks for delivery. Offer available while quantities last.

Your Privacy—The Reader Service is committed to protecting your privacy. Our Privacy Policy is available online at www.ReaderService.com or upon request from the Reader Service.

We make a portion of our mailing list available to reputable third parties that offer products we believe may interest you. If you prefer that we not exchange your name with third parties, or if you wish to clarify or modify your communication preferences, please visit us at www.ReaderService.com/consumerschoice or write to us at Reader Service Preference Service, P.O. Box 9062, Buffalo, NY 14240-9062. Include your complete name and address.

HPLP15

LARGER-PRINT BOOKS!
GET 2 FREE LARGER-PRINT NOVELS PLUS
2 FREE GIFTS!

⊕ HARLEQUIN®

INTRIGUE
BREATHTAKING ROMANTIC SUSPENSE

HILP15

READERSERVICE.COM

Manage your account online!

- Review your order history
- Manage your payments
- Update your address

> *We've designed the*
> *Reader Service website*
> *just for you.*

Enjoy all the features!

- Discover new series available to you, and read excerpts from any series.
- Respond to mailings and special monthly offers.
- Connect with favorite authors at the blog.
- Browse the Bonus Bucks catalog and online-only exculsives.
- Share your feedback.

Visit us at:
ReaderService.com